A TOUCH OF MAUVE

Larry Morrison Vaden

Copyright © 2021 by Larry Morrison Vaden

All rights reserved. No part of this publication may be reproduced, distributed or transmitted in any form or by any means, including photocopying, recording or other electronic or mechanical methods, without the prior written permission of the author, except in the case of brief quotations embodied in reviews and certain other non-commercial uses permitted by copyright law.

All oil paintings in the book are by Larry Morrison Vaden
Garage illustration by Mark Hobbs

Printed in the United States of America

Print ISBN: 978-1-953910-39-4
E-Book ISBN: 978-1-953910-40-0

Canoe Tree Press

4697 Main Street
Manchester Center, VT 05255

Canoe Tree Press is a division of DartFrog Books.

*To my mother, Epsie Pearl Vaden,
who dedicated her life to her husband and children;
my wife, Frances Vaden; and my children, Timothy
Vaden, Jonathan Vaden, and Deborah Barron.*

Acknowledgments

I have many people to thank for their support and help in writing this book. In a very real sense, this story grew out of my love of painting. It was through painting that I discovered I enjoyed expressing myself creatively.

I owe a great deal to my art teachers who patiently steered me through the hurdles that plague every artist on their journey to becoming a painter. I have original oil paintings by these artists that I would never part with, as their art is exceptional:

- International TV artist Gary Jenkins and his wife, Kathwren Jenkins, with whom I attended workshops for many years. I was privileged to receive their never-ending support and guidance in my work, and I am particularly grateful to them. Both of them are exceptional artists.
- National artist Mary Carole, whose expertise with the paint brush was awe-inspiring, and with whom I had the privilege of attending many workshops. She as well as Gary are masters of color and brushwork.
- National artist William Blackman, who patiently guided me through creating good and strong paintings. Bill has some of the most beautiful bluebonnet paintings I have ever seen.

I thank my typist, Saundra Gilmore, who patiently read my notes and scribbles and was able to produce a cohesive writing. She would sometimes provide advice or insight for the book, and I appreciated her input very much.

I am thankful for my two painting buddies, Brenda Gregory and Sharron Chester, who kept asking, "When are you going to finish the book?" I do admit that their constant nudging helped me to stay focused and helped me to finally finish it.

I also thank Mary Agnes Fuss, who did some partial editing of my manuscript and made some suggestions for changes that I included in my book, and whom I leaned on for encouragement. Agnes is a fine accomplished artist in her own right.

Prologue

Bernard was born into a family of eight children in the small town of Monterey, on the Cumberland Plateau in middle Tennessee. The family farmed for a living on nearly forty acres of land, and Bernard spent most of his early years working outdoors. The farm work was hard, and naturally he developed into a strapping young man. It was a simpler time, and the family enjoyed the fruits of their labor.

His mother, who was a lover of nature, made him aware of the beauty of his surroundings and taught him to enjoy, among other things, the blooming redbuds, the beautiful dogwoods, and the wild irises, lilies and daisies that bloomed along the edges of the fields.

After he graduated from high school, he served four years in the armed forces. It was during his time in the military that he met and married his wonderful and lovely wife Susan, who bore him three children. She was a great helpmate and a wonderful mother, and she was quite an asset to him in building two successful companies. They were living the American dream. The children had grown to be fine, upstanding citizens and were now pursuing their own dreams. Sometime later his wife became very ill and was diagnosed with cancer. Sadly, she was unresponsive to the many months of treatments and special care that was provided. She passed away quietly surrounded by her family.

He was distraught. How would he manage without her?

Time passed very slowly for Bernard; the years came and went, and he had great difficulty in shaking off his loneliness. Eventually he took up the hobby of oil painting and, to his surprise, found it to be a rewarding pastime. After much soul-searching he sold his companies and decided to do some traveling; perhaps a trip to Europe, where he and his wife had traveled when she was alive. It had been such a lovely experience, and he wanted to relive the trip that they had shared together. And, also, he might be able to do some painting while there.

He booked a flight to London, England, as a jumping-off point, only to discover that unexpected events lay ahead that would forever alter the course of his life.

Chapter 1

The Airbus started its descent through the depleting clouds over England. The weather was clearing, and the sun was beginning to shine, unlike the weather over Amsterdam where there was a thirty-minute delay due to severe crosswinds.

In Amsterdam, when the 747 did begin to land, only one set of wheels hit the landing strip first, making a tremendous jolt on one side of the plane. Then the plane settled down on the runway. After a change of planes with a two-hour layover, Bernard was on his way to London.

The English countryside was very picturesque with sheep and cattle grazing in the very green meadows. There were boats everywhere there was enough water to support them, even in small creeks and lakes. The sky was very blue with powder-puff clouds floating around. Whenever the plane flew through one of the clouds, the Airbus jarred, just like a car hitting a chughole in the street. This was caused by the cool temperature in the clouds. A bell started ringing, and the "fasten your seat belt" light came on. Just then Bernard, who always had a window seat when possible, noticed the scenery changing from country to suburban to city. The plane flew over the Thames River by Parliament, with the Big Ben tower and the Tower Bridge nearby. It was as though he had just had a private tour of London, by helicopter.

This time, the plane landed without incident at Heathrow Airport. The plane taxied up to the gate. Everyone disembarked, and Bernard followed the other passengers, not being sure of directions to the luggage pickup. Gathering his luggage and art gear, he headed to customs. Bernard showed his passport to the customs lady. She asked why he was there and did he have anything to declare. He said he was passing on through to Europe after a brief stay in London and he was bringing art supplies. She asked if they were for resale, as they looked new. He replied they were his personally and he would be using them as he traveled. She stamped his passport and allowed him through.

Bernard proceeded to the taxi area and hailed a taxi. He told the cab driver the hotel he wanted to go to. The cabby opened the door and being indifferent, pointed where to put the luggage. With no help from the cabby, Bernard loaded his own luggage and gear.

When they arrived at the hotel, the cabby stood aside and let Bernard unload his own luggage. He paid the cabby and left no tip. Luckily, there was a bellhop there to take the luggage to the desk where he checked in. Showing his passport and credit card, he picked up his key, and the bellhop took his luggage to his room. He tipped the bellhop, then returned to the lobby to pick up a newspaper to check out local rentals of apartments or houses. This would be cheaper than staying in a pricey hotel and would allow him more freedom to move around.

The following morning, after a quick breakfast, he bought a local map at a newsstand and began to walk the area and check out some local rentals. He had taken his camera with him to take photos of interest around the area near his hotel. A fair distance from his hotel, his eye caught some color behind a hedge just off the main road. Getting closer, he pushed his way into the hedgerow for a better look. On the other side of the hedge, he saw an older woman bent over, hoeing and chopping weeds in a garden of flowers and vegetables. Pulling the thick hedge back as much as possible, Bernard stuck his head through a small hole in the hedge. Seeing such a beautiful flower garden and seeing a chance to take photos of beautiful deep-colored flowers, he called out to the woman.

"Hello, may I come into your garden and take some photos of your flowers?"

The lady straightened up and looked around the garden but could not see anyone. She then returned to chopping weeds.

Again, Bernard called out and said, "May I come into your garden and take some photos?"

She raised up again and looked around but did not see anyone. She yelled out loudly, "Where are you?"

Bernard yelled back, "Over here in the hedgerow."

The lady looked toward where the voice came from, then spotted Bernard with only his head protruding through the hedge. She began to laugh a side-splitting laugh, shaking her head at just a human head sticking out of the hedgerow. When she finished laughing, she asked, "What was that again?"

Bernard replied, "I would like to take photos of your beautiful flowers."

"Yes, that you may," said the lady.

Bernard asked, "How do I get into the garden?"

She replied, "Go down and come in through the garage. The door is open."

Bernard retrieved himself from the hedge and walked down the walk to an old green garage. The garage, built in the 1920s out of wood clapboard siding, was constructed with a gable at each end and another gable coming out the center overhanging a drive-through to gas up cars. This allowed cars to be filled with gas on either side of the gas pump and stay out of the weather. The old hand-crank pump was still standing where it was installed. The pump was gravity-fed out of a large glass bowl on top of the pump. The two newer-style electric pumps had been removed and were standing against the garage wall.

The main garage had a wide single sliding door on the right side to allow vehicles to enter and be repaired. Under the front gable was the customer and personnel door.

To the left was a large display window with a sign reading "To Let." Bernard entered through the personnel door, which had two brass bells tied onto a small red and green rope that rang when he opened the door to announce one's presence. Bernard continued through the large display room to a kitchen and living area with a table and chairs and a side table. Passing through the kitchen area, he went out the back door to the garden.

The lady, possibly in her middle eighties, was standing and leaning with one hand on the hoe and the other on her hip, tired from chopping weeds. Bernard took a picture of her leaning on the hoe.

Bernard said, "You have a beautiful garden here."

"Thank you," said the lady.

Bernard introduced himself. "My name is Bernard Anderson, and I am pleased to meet you."

The lady in the garden said, "My name is Betty Putnam, but you may call me Betsey. That is what they called me in school, and it stuck with me, and I am pleased to meet you."

Bernard said, "I was walking down the sidewalk, and the beautiful colors caught my eye. You have the most beautiful flowers here." He continued, "The colors here in England are much more intense than back home in the South. The heat from the sun bleaches them out in just a few days."

Mrs. Putnam replied, "I thought you were a Yank when I heard you talking." She laughed.

"Well, not a Yank but a Tennessee hillbilly," Bernard said. "You must put in a lot of work keeping this garden looking so beautiful."

Betsey replied, "At my age, that is about all I have to look forward to. It's a lot of hard work digging in dirt; however, I really enjoy it."

Bernard said, "I noticed you have living quarters in the garage, and you have a sign on the door of the garage, 'To Let.' Do you rent that out, and if so, how much do you rent it for?"

"Yes, I rent it; it is not much of an apartment. A man of your caliber might not want to live in a place like that. After you take your pictures, I will show it to you and see if you are still interested in it."

Bernard, thanking her, excused himself and continued to take photographs of the flowers and blooming shrubs. He saw she had a pond off the back porch of the two-story house where Betsey lived. The house had an upper balcony and a lower porch that ran the full length of the rear of the house, and the koi pond was just off the porch at the edge of the yard and garden.

When Bernard was through taking photos, he asked Betsey if she would show him the garage living quarters. Betsey walked out of the garden and to the little green garage and leaned the hoe against the garden side of the garage. She invited Bernard inside the garage. Betsey asked Bernard, "Where did you say you were from?"

Bernard replied, "I'm from a small town called Monterey in the state of Tennessee. It's located in the middle of the United States, east of the Mississippi River. You have a nice place here with beautiful surroundings."

"Yes, I have lived here most of my life except when I was married. My father built this place, and I was born here. It used to be on the main road, but they rerouted the road, and now we are on a side street. That is why the station eventually went out of business. Dad was ready to retire anyway. They have built up all around me, and not a month goes by that a realtor doesn't come by and knock on my door to see if I will sell. My dad built the garage in the '20s but had to close it down because of his health and decline of business. He had some living quarters added on and hired a handy man to look after the place and keep it up. After he died, I moved back home because my husband had already passed away. I hired a housekeeper to look after my mother, and she lived there until my mother died. It has been empty until now. I thought I would rent it to supplement my income, as all I get is an old-age pension. It has two baths and a kitchen, and a small eating area with a table and chairs. It has a small gas stove and refrigerator. There is a bedroom with a twin bed, dresser, and chest of drawers. That is where the other bath is. That was added later when we hired the handy man. It is not much, but it is clean."

Bernard asked, "How much is the rent?"

She replied, "Two hundred and fifty pounds a month, and that includes utilities. You look big and strong. If you will help me with my heavy work occasionally, you can have it for two hundred pounds. I will wash the bed linens and towels once a week. If you want to, you can throw in your washables, and I will wash them also."

Bernard asked if the large room that had the big window went with it.

"You can have the whole building as far as I am concerned. That was the salesroom where they kept automotive products."

Bernard said, "I will take it." He reached into his waistband, pulled out express checks and British pound notes, and paid Betsey for the first month's rent. He asked her when he could move in.

She said, "You can move in tomorrow if you like."

Betsey asked Bernard what type of work he did. He told her he was retired and had sold his businesses, and that he was retracing a tour he and his wife had gone on when she was alive. He told her he did artwork for a hobby and flowers were his main subject.

Betsey laughed and said, "This is the right place for that."

Bernard said, "I will be here the first thing in the morning."

Betsey replied, "I am going to do some more dusting and tidying up for you so it will be clean for you by the first thing in the morning."

Bernard bid her good day. Leaving, he said he would return around eight a.m. Mrs. Putnam assured him she would be waiting for him.

Bernard returned to his hotel and repacked his clothes. The next day after a quick breakfast, he checked out and called a taxi. The ride was short, but it kept Bernard from making three trips to move everything to the little green garage. Mrs. Putnam was watching for him from the two-story balcony.

Seeing the taxi arrive, she went down from the house and through the back door of the garage and opened the front door for Bernard, making it easier for him to bring in his supplies. Mrs. Putnam bid him good morning and gave him the keys to the garage. She asked him if he needed any help. Bernard replied no, he thought he had it under control. She assured him the place had been re-cleaned and told him if he needed anything, he should just come up to the house and ring the bell.

Bernard put away his clothes in the dresser and chest of drawers. He hung his shirts and pants in the closet. He looked around to decide where was the best place to set up his easel and paint supplies. He moved the side table to where his back would be toward the window. He set up his easel beside the table and started unpacking his brushes and colors, then hung his apron on the easel. He unpacked his CD player with the earphones. He then looked for his CDs but could not find them. The last he remembered was putting them on the dresser back home while he was packing. That is one thing he would have to buy here in London. He always listened to soft music while painting. He believed good music leads to inspiration while painting.

He had to go out and buy groceries, so he decided he would check out a music store as well and buy some canvases and paint thinner he was not allowed to bring on the plane.

Bernard walked down to the two-story white house, passing a café table with two chairs. The path was made with flagstone and was very ambling through the garden of flowers. Bernard twisted the old bell that was built into the door. After a slight delay, Mrs. Putnam came to the door and greeted him. She asked how things were going. Bernard said fine, but needed directions to the grocery store and a music store that sold records.

After getting directions, he walked on toward the grocer but decided to pass up the grocery store and buy his food last to prevent spoilage. He would go to the music store first.

After entering the music store, he asked the clerk where the easy listening music was kept. The clerk showed him in which aisle they were. Bernard was oblivious to the music playing over the store speakers. To him, that was just background noise. While he was looking through the volumes of CDs for easy listening, he heard one of the most beautiful and unusual voices coming from the overhead store speakers. He quit looking for his easy listening music and just stared off into space, listening to that beautiful voice. He was completely mesmerized by her voice. After the music finished, he asked the clerk who was the lady he had heard singing over the store speakers. The clerk replied that it was Lilly Montgomery, one of England's finest singers. Bernard asked where her recordings were. The clerk took him over to the rack where her CDs were displayed. Bernard thumbed through the CD albums and picked three by Lilly and three easy listening. Bernard had forgotten about the art supplies he needed, and after paying the clerk, he asked where he could find the art store. The clerk told him the general directions and also drew him a map on a small piece of paper so he would not get lost.

Bernard continued to the art store and purchased some canvases, odorless thinner, and linseed oil, items he was not allowed to carry on the airplane. Finding he could not carry this and his groceries, he decided to take everything back to the little green garage. After unloading his purchases, he went to the grocery store. Bernard picked out food he could prepare quickly and not have to spend time cooking. He picked out lunch meats, milk, bread, cheeses, and crackers, topped off with a bottle of wine, some canned sodas, and flavored carbonated drinks.

Arriving back at his domain, Bernard put the food away in the refrigerator and cabinets. He could hardly wait to hear Lilly's voice on the CDs. Tearing off the plastic cover on one of the CDs, he inserted it into his player and put on his apron and earphones. He put the player into the center pocket of his painting apron, then turned on the CD player and listened to the beautiful voice of Lilly Montgomery. Her lilting voice created just the right mood for setting up his painting arrangement.

He walked down the path to the two-story white house which sat at a ninety-degree angle of the little green garage overlooking the koi pond and garden. Bernard twisted the knob of the bell in the door. When Betsey came to the door, Bernard asked her if it would be all right to pick some flowers from the garden to paint.

Betsey replied, "Oh, for heaven's sake, pick all you want anytime."

Bernard thanked her, then returned to get a knife from his kitchen and began to cut a bouquet of flowers from the garden. He took them inside and put them in an old fruit jar that had been sitting on a shelf for ages. He filled the jar half full of water and arranged the flowers for the best effect to paint. After setting up his subject matter in a desirable composition, he began to paint as he listened to Lilly singing on the CD player.

Evening came too soon for Bernard. The light outside began to fade too quickly for him to continue the painting, and the inside light was not suitable either. Bernard thought, well, this will have to wait until tomorrow.

Making himself a sandwich and sitting down at the café table outside with some chips and a glass of wine, he continued playing Lilly's songs. After eating, he continued to sit there playing her CDs until dark.

Going inside and appreciating her beautiful singing, he decided to write Lilly a letter and tell her how much he enjoyed her singing. Remembering he did not have any stationery, he made a special trip to the drugstore nearby. He decided on a package of ten tan parchment envelopes, each with writing paper that folded in the middle. While there, he bought a CD player with external speakers attached so he could share the music with Betsey.

After entering the garage, he locked up for the night. He pulled up a chair to the kitchen table and opened the package of parchment stationery. Playing one of Lilly's CDs, he began to write: "Dear Lilly, ..." He ended the letter with "I hope you have a wonderful day ... Bernard." Before he signed the letter, however, it occurred to him he might not sign his real name but use a fictitious one instead. While he was thinking and trying to decide how he would sign it, he was looking at his art supplies. And then it occurred to him: "I know what I will do; I will sign it 'Art.' That way she will probably think my name is Arthur and will never know from whom it came."

Satisfied he had done the right thing, he placed the letter in the envelope and addressed it to the fan mail address on the CD brochure. He walked down to the mailbox on the street he had noticed while gathering supplies.

The next day, Bernard began work on his floral paintings.

Betsey came by to check on his progress and asked him to move a waste container to the street for her when he had time, adding that there was no hurry.

Bernard said, "Sure, let me finish these leaves, and I will be right out."

Betsey was interested in his progress and was very impressed with his art ability. She was becoming a one-woman cheerleader for him.

Meanwhile, two days later, on a Friday evening, Lilly Montgomery, her boyfriend James, Lilly's cousin Mary, and Mary's boyfriend were dining at a posh restaurant in London. They were enjoying an expensive meal of lobster, filet mignon, fish and shrimp with vegetables and wine. Near the end of the meal, Lilly asked Mary if she wanted to accompany her to the ladies' room. Mary said, "Sure," and they both left carrying their purses.

Coming out of the restroom and walking down the aisle behind a divider that separated foot traffic from the dining area, Lilly happened to look over the divider near their table only to overhear James tell the waitress, "No, we are not serious; she is just a friend."

Lilly stopped in her tracks and asked Mary, "Did you hear that?"

Mary said, "Yes, but I wish I had not."

The waitress seemed to be enjoying James as much as he was her.

Having been through two divorces, Lilly was incensed by what he said. Some men think women are stupid. Lilly told Mary she was leaving and would take a taxi back to their condominium. Mary asked Lilly what she should tell James.

Lilly said, "Tell the bastard whatever you want. I am through with him. He has been nothing but a freeloader anyway."

Lilly stormed out of the restaurant and hailed a taxi back to her condominium. Mary went back to their table alone and told James Lilly had gone home.

James asked, "Why? Was she sick?"

"No," replied Mary, "she heard what you said to the waitress."

"Oh, no!" replied James.

With that, they settled up the bill and left James to find his own way home.

It was a long ride back to the condominium for Lilly. After two divorces, she could not tolerate this type of behavior anymore. She was thinking that this is the curse of being rich and famous. How can you tell who is along for the ride or who is serious when you try to find someone to love? Men lead you along and lie to you as if it is a game. It seems that all of them are looking for a free meal ticket and a good time, caring nothing about the women they discard along the way.

She arrived at the condominium, and while she was trying to unlock the door she heard the phone ringing. Once inside, she picked up the phone, and it was James. She quickly told him it was over and to never call her again, then hung up the phone and unplugged it from the wall.

Lilly changed into her nightgown and started watching television. Reading was out of the question, because she was too mad to concentrate. She just wanted to get her mind off the evening.

An hour later, Mary came in and said James seemed to be upset.

"I know," said Lilly, "I talked to him and told him never to call again. He is not upset at losing me, he is upset at losing a free ride and a free meal ticket."

They sat talking for a while and turned in for the night. Lilly tossed and turned most of the night from being upset.

Lilly lay in bed longer than usual the next morning, still upset from the previous night. She finally dressed, and about ten a.m., Mary came in with the mail and handed Lilly her mail. The one that caught her eye was the tan parchment envelope marked "Personal." She reached for the letter opener, sliced the envelope open, and began to read.

Dear Lilly,

Today I experienced a most joyful time of my life. I thought I must be in heaven when I heard your beautiful voice for the first time. I found it hard to believe an earthling could have such a wonderful voice. I stood mesmerized in the music store, no longer aware of my surroundings. You have the most beautiful voice I have ever heard. When I saw your picture on the CD package, I was astonished that you were such a beautiful woman. I feel honored to have lived to hear your voice. When you sing, a person is transfixed in their mind oblivious of anything around them except the beauty of your voice, forgetting their troubles and sorrows. I wrote you a poem; I hope you will like it. It is called "Lilly."

Lilly

Today I came upon a beautiful lily
A lily growing in an open field
It was such a beautiful lily

> I could hardly believe it was real
> I started to pluck the lily and take
> It home with me
> But it was such a beautiful lily
> I decided to let it be
> To let it multiply and grow
> So, to others let its beauty show.

I hope you have a wonderful day.
Your loyal fan,
Art

Mary came back in with some more mail. Lilly spoke up and said, "Well, here is someone who loves me for who I am." Lilly laughed. "He even wrote me a personal poem," Lilly added, handing the letter to Mary. Mary read the letter and said, "Wow, you'd better watch out!" and laughed. The letter lifted Lilly's spirits. With a smile still on her face, she placed the letter back into the envelope and laid it by her purse because of the poem in the letter. She would reread it sometime.

Bernard was beginning to settle into life at his garage abode. He next painted roses with daisies. When Betsey came by to see what he was painting, she liked it so much she offered Bernard a free month's rent for it. She said she wanted to send it to her sister in Birmingham. Bernard, knowing Betsey needed the money, said no, but she could have it for twenty pounds. He knew this was more in line with what she could afford. Betsey said that was not enough, but she agreed with him for twenty pounds. He put the finishing touches on the painting and set it aside to dry for Betsey.

He finished another one of red roses on a white picket fence and placed it in the large window with a sign that read "Art For Sale." All the while he was painting, he used the small CD player he kept in his apron pocket, with earphones for a better sound effect. When he and Betsey both listened, he used the CD player with external speakers. He took the large CD player and set it on the back porch of Betsey's house so she could also hear Lilly sing. He kept telling Betsey what a wonderful singer Lilly was. While painting, Bernard said, "Good music sets the mood and makes the painting go better, and it gives you more inspiration." At least it turned him into a mood more conducive to painting.

Pink Roses on Red

Betsey stopped by on her way to the garden to check on his paintings. When Bernard needed a break, he went outside and helped Betsey with whatever chores she happened to be doing. He sometimes just pulled weeds out of the flowers. Having been raised on a farm, this was one job for which he was well qualified. Bernard continued to do her heavy lifting for her. She was very thankful to have him around.

Betsey teased him from time to time, telling him every woman needs a man like him. Bernard said, "Thanks for the compliment, but I have had enough women to last a lifetime," and laughed.

Bernard went back inside to paint. He started by putting on Lilly's music to paint by. On hearing her lovely voice again, he decided to write her another letter, thinking to himself that she may have a husband or boyfriend, but that it did not matter because he was using a fake name. No one would ever know, and only she would know how he felt about her.

He began, "Dear Lilly, I am still enjoying your singing..." and signed the finished letter "Art." Bernard delayed his painting and made a special effort to walk down the street and mail the letter, then returned to his painting.

Bernard had planned on staying only a short time in London but decided he was not in a hurry. It was quiet and laid back, and he enjoyed Betsey's company. Some evenings when he was not too tired, he would take Betsey down to the Horse and Saddle Pub and treat her to a fresh cooked meal. He was interested in people's lives from another country. He would always ask her questions about growing up. Betsey did not like for him to pay rent and buy her meals, but he did anyway. One of the reasons he decided to stay longer was to visit some of the museums. London had some of the best, and Tate museum was supposed to be one of the best in the world.

About three days later at Lilly's condominium. Mary brought in the mail, and there was another parchment envelope marked "Personal." Mary handed the mail to Lilly. Lilly reached for the parchment envelope first. Retrieving the letter opener, she sliced the envelope open. Lilly, being more inquisitive than the last time, took the letter from the envelope and began to read.

> *Dear Lilly,*
>
> *I am still enjoying your singing. You have a most unusual voice. It is so beautiful and soothing. You do not realize how much your singing is enjoyed by everyone. I am so touched by your singing that I am sending you another poem I wrote just for you. It is called "Lilly on the Path."*

Lilly on the Path
Walking along a wandering path I see
A beautiful girl that is looking toward me.
She is as beautiful as a lily in the mow
She has a beautiful smile and facial glow
As she nears me, she slows her pace
To allow me to see her pretty face
With eyes of light cerulean blue
And lips as moist as the morning dew.
Walking by I asked who she may be
Lilly, she said, and what about thee.
My name is Art, as we drifted apart
She had disarmed me and stolen my heart.

> I hope to live for another day
> When that beautiful girl walks this way
> No beautiful flower did ever I see
> As Lilly who looked and smiled at me.

Have a wonderful day. I am always thinking of you.
Art

After Lilly finished reading the letter she began to smile. The letter had a personal effect on Lilly, making her feel better about herself even though she had never met the man. Since Mary had teased her about the first letter, Lilly could not wait to call Mary to come and read the letter.

Mary came in, then Lilly, grinning, handed the letter to Mary. Mary finished reading the letter and said, "Wow, he's getting more personal. Perhaps you do have a man in your life." Lilly just smiled, and Mary said, "I wonder who he is?"

"I do too," said Lilly. "His name must be Arthur because he signs his name Art, which is short for Arthur. He does not leave a return address that we can trace back. He must not want his identity known."

Lilly read the letter again, especially the poem. She then put the letter back in the envelope and then in her purse with the other letter, leaving a warm feeling toward "Arthur."

Meanwhile, Bernard sold one of his paintings to a passerby for a modest sum. Betsey told two of her friends about his art. They came by and were very impressed, and he sold one to each of them.

Yellow Roses and Cosmos

He continued to help Betsey to give himself a break from painting from time to time and to refresh himself. He was developing a closeness to Betsey, as she would often cut flowers and take to a nearby nursing home to cheer the people up. He thought Betsey had a heart of gold that was making his stay there a lot more pleasant.

Bernard made a trip to an art museum in downtown London to garner some ideas, broaden his knowledge of art, and find inspiration. He paid special attention to how the people dressed and intermingled with each other in London. He also paid attention to the types of cars they drove. All in all, it was an educational experience.

On returning home from his excursion, Bernard felt the

urge to play some more of Lilly's CDs, and he was aware that he was becoming more and more attached to this beautiful singer. Her voice had a special warmth that drew Bernard to her and removed any loneliness from a person being away from home.

Still listening to Lilly's recordings, he decided to write her another letter.

"Dear Lilly," he began, "I am still enjoying your singing and beautiful voice." He ended, "I hope you are having a wonderful day. I wonder at times what you may be doing at that particular time. Thinking of you, Love, Your loyal fan, Art."

Bernard went down the street and dropped the letter in the postal box. Then he went back to painting and helping Betsey. He enjoyed taking Betsey to the pub, buying her supper, and listening to her tales of growing up in London, attending school, dating, and what they did for entertainment. Some of the stories were hilarious, as Betsey was not embarrassed by her behavior as a youth.

A few days later, Mary brought in the daily mail and handed Lilly another yellowish beige envelope marked "Personal." Lilly could not wait. She grabbed the letter opener and sliced open the envelope. Unfolding the letter, she began to read.

Dear Lilly,

I am still enjoying your singing and beautiful voice. I stand in awe when hearing your singing. I think you are the most wonderful singer in the world. I think of you and listen to your recordings several times a day. I go to sleep at night playing one of your recordings. I wrote another poem for you. A poet I am not, but these are my feelings that I send to you.

Lilly of My Dreams
I dream of you and your lovely hair
Your lovely lips and face so fair
Your wonderful voice and eyes of blue
There is no other woman as lovely as you.
I wish to be the one by your side
To walk with you and show my pride
I try to tell you how much I care
I reach for you, but you are not there.
I search and search and cannot find
The beautiful girl that is always on my mind
You are gone from me and I could scream
Then I awake to find it is only a dream
I hope someday my dream comes true
That I can share my life and be with you.

I hope you are having a wonderful day. Thinking of you,
Love,
Your loyal fan,
Art

Lilly thought to herself, someone in this world cares enough for me to write and send me personal poems. Lilly called Mary and had her read the letter. After reading the letter, Mary smiled and said, "I wish someone cared enough for me to make up poems and send them to me." Lilly tried to downplay the letters as though they were nothing to her.

But once the seed is planted, if nurtured it begins to sprout roots, grow, and take hold.

Lilly tried to play down the fact that the letters were beginning to occupy her thoughts during the day and that they were, in some ways, filling a void in her life. Mary was still wondering who he was. Lilly was also wondering. She said, "He never leaves a return address. It will be my luck that he is ninety years old and uses a walker." They both burst out laughing.

Bernard filled his days painting, helping Betsey in the garden, and listening to Lilly's recordings. Betsy's flowers were beautiful, and he enjoyed painting them. He also spent a lot of time visiting museums in London. But in spite of these distractions, Lilly was foremost on his mind nearly all the time.

Finding himself, one evening, in a contemplative mood, and being preoccupied with thoughts of Lilly each hour of every day, he decided to send her another poem. He wrote: "Dear Lilly, You are forever on my mind. I find it strange that I could fall in love with someone I have never met. It is your beauty and singing that capture me. I have written you another poem," and ended with, "Always thinking of you ... Your biggest admirer, Love, Art."

Bernard put the letter in the envelope and mailed it at the postal box. He tried to think of other things. He spent some time with Betsey in the garden. That evening they both went down to the Horse and Saddle Pub for supper.

Two days later, Mary brought in the mail as Lilly was watching television. Mary handed her the parchment envelope. Lilly smiled and went to her side table to retrieve her letter opener. She opened the envelope and began to read:

Dear Lilly,

You are forever on my mind. I find it strange that I could fall in love with someone I have never met. It is your beauty and singing that capture me. I have written you another poem. It is called "My Dream."

My Dream

Falling in love with someone you never see
How in heaven and earth can this be
It is listening to your voice as you sing
that puts me in a trance, and I begin to dream
Of our walking together on the willow green
Down the path to the willow stream
Down the path to where the weeping willows grow
With swaying branches as the winds blow
With birds fluttering and singing in the trees
Enjoying the spring and April breeze
Walking hand in hand with the girl I adore
We cross the stream to the other shore
With our lives that are now born anew
I give my heart and my love to you
We walk through the spring flowers growing wild
You devour me with your beautiful smile
Those cerulean blue eyes have disarmed me
I am charmed by those beautiful eyes, you see
You sing a song to me to show your love
With a voice that surely came from above
With all your natural beauty and heavenly bliss
I wrap my arms around you and give you a kiss
As all poems must come to an end

I wonder when we meet, where should I begin?

Always thinking of you ...
Your biggest admirer, Love,
Art

Later Mary came back in and saw Lilly staring at the letter. Mary asked, "What is wrong?"

"I don't know; he is getting serious." Lilly handed Mary the letter.

After Mary read the letter she said, "I think he is really in love with you."

Lilly said, "Yes, but I can't do anything about it if I don't know who and where he is." When Mary was not watching, Lilly read the poems over and over again, wondering who Art was.

By the time Lilly had gotten this letter, Bernard was busy writing another letter to Lilly. After a few more days, another letter arrived at Lilly's condominium. Mary sorted the mail and gave Lilly her special letter. Lilly, eager to read it, sliced open the envelope and read:

Dear Lilly,
My life is consumed with your singing and thinking of you. I would surely like to meet you some day. I play your music as I work. This poem is called "Your Voice."

Your Voice
I love to hear your voice when you sing
Your voice is so smooth and so serene.

The notes you sing seem to float in the air
With a voice so soft and sweet none can compare
Your songs seem to be calling only to me
They affect everything I do and see
I hold on to every note and every refrain
Hoping my love for you is not in vain
Your voice is like a butterfly floating in the air
Sung so soft and graceful, so debonair.
So, with every song that you sing
Think of me and the love that I bring.
With such a beautiful voice you do sing
Such a lovely voice that would surely entice a king.

Forever yours,
Love,
Art

These letters and poems began to take hold of Lilly's thinking. You can only feel good toward someone who tells you they love you. After a while Mary came back in, and Lilly handed her the letter. After Mary read the letter, she asked Lilly, "What do you think?"

Lilly replied, "The poems are beginning to get to me. I just wish he would show his face."

At the little green garage, Bernard was sitting outside in the café chair with an empty coffee cup and listening to Lilly through his earphones. It was getting dark, and he decided to go inside and write Lilly another letter. After all, he would not be staying much longer in London, and he decided to use up all the envelopes writing Lilly. He went inside, turned on the lights, and wrote Lilly another letter, which he posted that night.

A few days later, Mary handed Lilly another letter. Lilly opened the envelope and read:

Dear Lilly,
I am still playing your recordings. You have such a beautiful voice. I am sending you another poem. It is called "Wonderful Lilly."

Wonderful Lilly

Anyone would find you wonderful to love
With a voice so soft and sweet as a morning dove
With eyes that sparkle like reflections in the rain
With lips as soft and moist as a glass of champagne
With cheeks that reflect their beauty in the light
Blonde hair that frames your face in a beautiful sight
I love to hear your voice when you sing
Like a meadowlark announcing the arrival of spring
I cannot stop thinking of everything about you
Of the songs you sing and the things you do.
Your smile would disarm the hardest of hearts
I long for the day when I can call you sweetheart.

Love you still,
Art

Lilly called Mary and let her read the letter. Mary said, "I wish the best for you, and if he turns out to be a good fit for you, you deserve it. Someday we will find out who he is. I just hope he is not married."

Lilly replied, "Yes, as I am getting my hopes up, that would be a bummer."

Meanwhile, Bernard was spending his days talking to Betsey and painting while listening to Lilly sing. He painted koi, birds, and some florals. He wrote another poem to Lilly and mailed it immediately, in the postal box down the street.

A few days later, the tan envelope arrived at Lilly's mailbox, marked, as usual, "Personal." Lilly read the letter and shared it with Mary. Mary said, "It's nice, but I wouldn't get my hopes up because there are too many obstacles in the way to make it come true." It read:

Dear Lilly,
I am hoping this letter finds you in good spirits. I enjoy your singing so much. I wrote you another poem. It is called "A Kiss."

A Kiss

When you sing, it is plain to see
I pretend the words are just for me
Though you may wish I did not exist
It is your beautiful voice I cannot resist.
Melodies with which you melt my heart
though life's journey keeps us apart
I not only love the beauty of your voice
Falling in love with you is my choice
To hold you and love you is my dream
I hold your existence in the highest esteem
If I could only take my fingers and touch your face
It would be heaven if we could embrace

It would be great to seal our love in wonderful bliss
If only I could softly steal a lovely kiss.

Until we meet.
Love,
Art

A few days later, Bernard sent another letter to Lilly. Mary separated the mail as usual and gave the tan parchment envelope to Lilly. Lilly, as eager as ever, opened the envelope and started reading.

Dear Lilly,
I am sending you another poem, and I hope you like it. It is called "Lilly in the Garden."

Lilly in the Garden
As I hear your singing your voice carries me away
It leaves me with a feeling that carries me through the day
So, I walked into the garden to see what I could find
Finding a beautiful flower was the last thing on my mind
I walked around some thistles to keep away from thorns
I walked into some cockleburs and all I did was scorn
I continued on my trek and walked amongst the weeds
All I gathered on this trip was a pocket full of seeds
Then I saw some color from behind some debris
I pulled away the rubbish to see what I could see
There amongst the weeds was a beautiful Lilly growing all alone
It was such a gorgeous Lilly, I claimed it for my own
I cut the weeds from the Lilly to keep it away from harm

So that I could see the Lilly and enjoy its wonderful charms
I made an oath to the Lilly that I will always be
The one to look after it and keep it company
If a human this beautiful Lilly could become
I would ask her to marry me and we could live as one.

You still sing me to sleep every night.
Loving you,
Art

Lilly showed the letter to Mary, and Mary said, "Such a sweet poem. You know he is proposing to you, don't you?"

Lilly was beginning to think Art was going to introduce himself very soon. This was very encouraging, because she had built up an affection for him because of his writings. Mary said, "It appears he loves you. I hope he doesn't turn out to be a dud."

Lilly put the letter with the other seven, tied them with the ribbon, and put them in her purse.

Chapter 2

Lilly, being famous, had to be careful when and where she went out. However, on occasion, Lilly and Mary would take a foray out into the public. This gave them a chance to mix with the rest of the population. In doing so, they would don large hats or scarves and sunglasses.

This was the apparel they were wearing when they decided to go out to a boot sale. In America, this is known as a flea market. There were so many people and cars that they had to park down a side street near an old green garage, not even paying attention to its existence. Having to walk a few blocks, they arrived at a large array of people and material objects.

They had no plans to buy anything, just to look at the strange items that people had to sell. Lilly was able to tour the hodgepodge of thousands of items without being noticed. Even though they enjoyed refreshments during the tour, they became tired of walking and decided it was time to return to the car with the few Hummel figurines they had purchased.

While almost to their car, Lilly noticed the paintings in the window of the old garage. "Mary, look at those beautiful flowers."

Mary, looking around, said, "I don't see any flowers."

Lilly said, Those paintings in the windows of that old garage."

Mary replied, "Oh."

Lilly said, "Let's go over there and see them." Having seen the sign in the window, "Art for Sale," they went to the front of the garage, where a sign on the door said "Open." They turned the doorknob and went into the garage, with two bronze bells ringing their entry. They walked to the center of the empty front room and, not seeing anyone, said, "Hello, anyone here?"

Bernard was in the backroom, painting and finishing a few brush strokes. He answered, "Just a minute." Wiping off his brush with a paper towel, he laid the brush down on the table, then got up and came around the corner and stopped dead in his tracks. There was the woman of his dreams standing there with Mary, both holding large hats and sunglasses in their hands. Lilly was even more beautiful than her photograph. She just smiled, and when she did, her beautiful, full crimson lips curled up in such a way that reminded him of the way rose petals would curl up at the edges. Her face was like porcelain and without blemish, reminding him of the dolls he had seen girls playing with in his youth. They stared at each other for a moment. He was looking at her blue eyes that drew him in like a magnet. Her beautiful blonde hair framed and accentuated her beautiful face, while her slim waist and ample breasts accentuated her beautiful body. The situation seemed so unreal. Bernard, in a daze, wondered to himself how she found out that he was the one sending her those letters, and whether she had come to tell him off and stop him sending them. Unable to speak, he just stood there trying to think.

Lilly and Mary started giggling because he was speechless,

and they thought it was because he has recognized Lilly as a well-known singer, which he had, but for a completely different reason. Finally, to break the silence, Lilly said, "We would like to see your paintings."

Bernard, with his brain still in a fog, seemed not to know what they were talking about. "Paintings?" he asked. Here Bernard was standing knee deep in an art studio, and he seemed to know nothing about paintings.

Lilly and Mary, still snickering, said, "Yes," pointing to the ones in the window for sale.

Now Bernard's brain was beginning to thaw. "Oh yes," he said, somewhat relieved. He proceeded to take the paintings from the window and said, "If you will, come through here to the outside so that you can see them better. There is better light out there." Bernard went through the dining area, where he painted, carrying the paintings out the back door to the café table and chairs. Lilly and Mary followed and saw where Bernard was painting. Bernard set a painting in each chair in a shaded area to prevent glare on the paintings. Lilly and Mary raved about the two paintings. Lilly liked the one with the two yellow roses best. Lilly asked, "What is the price of the painting?" Bernard named a reasonable price of eighty pounds because of the prestige of her owning one of his paintings. Lilly said she would take the rose painting. He took both paintings back inside and placed the rose painting in a large plastic bag. While he was doing that, Mary and Lilly were looking admiringly at the irises he was painting on the easel.

A TOUCH OF MAUVE

Yellow Roses on White

Icelandic Poppies

Lilly asked Bernard if he taught painting. Bernard replied yes, he had taught art some in the past, but just the basic stuff. Lilly said, "I have always wanted to paint but couldn't for the obvious reasons. I need to disguise myself and cannot go just anywhere and, in the past, I did not have time to paint. I happen to have some free time for two months, and I would like to try. This place would be perfect as I would not be seen going and coming or have to worry about talking to people and signing autographs. What do you charge for lessons, and how long is each lesson?"

Bernard said, "Twenty-five pounds for a half day or fifty pounds for a full day. We could do all day, which would be a little rough, or half days, which would be easier."

Lilly said she preferred half days.

Bernard said, "We could start at eight and go until noon."

Lilly replied, "That would be too early, as I like to sleep in."

Bernard said, "How about ten until two-thirty or three?"

"That will be fine," said Lilly. "Do I need to bring any painting supplies, as I don't have any?"

"No," said Bernard, "you can use mine."

"When could I start?" asked Lilly.

"You can start tomorrow, which is Monday," replied Bernard.

"That will be fine with me. I will be here at ten a.m., and I am really looking forward to it," said Lilly, reaching for her painting.

Bernard quickly grabbed the painting and said, "I will take it to your car for you." They all went out the front door to the beautiful powder-blue Jaguar sedan that Lilly was driving. Bernard placed the painting on the driver's side with the back of the painting leaning against the driver's seat. That way, if she stopped or accelerated too quickly, it would stay in place.

Lilly said, "By the way, I didn't introduce my friend and secretary, Mary Williams, and I think you know who I am," said Lilly, smiling.

Bernard turned red in the face and nodded acknowledgment to Lilly, with a big smile on his face. Bernard introduced himself, saying "I am Bernard Anderson."

Lilly said, "You are not from here, are you? You sound like a Yank."

Bernard replied, "Well, I am not a Yank, and I hail from Monterey, Tennessee."

"Where is that?" asked Lilly.

"It is located in the mid-eastern part of the United States."

Getting into the car with Mary, Lilly said, "I will be here at ten a.m."

Bernard said, "Wear old clothes."

When they drove away, Lilly and Mary were still laughing. Mary said, "Lilly, did you ever see a person at such a loss for words as he was? You sure made an impression on him, poor fellow," not knowing the real reason.

Bernard stood there and watched them drive away. Walking back into the garage, he sat down by his easel thinking about what had just transpired. It seemed so unreal. If he had not been a participant, he would not have believed it himself. He got up out of his seat and walked as if in a daydream down the garden path to Betsey's house.

Betsey was on the porch preparing green beans that she had picked from her garden. Betsey noticed he seemed as if he was in a daze. Betsey asked Bernard if anything was wrong, because she knew something was bothering him. He pulled up a chair and sat down next to Betsey. Betsey asked Bernard, "Are you all right?"

Bernard sat silent for a minute and said, "Betsey, you know Lilly, the woman on the CD."

"Yes," said Betsey.

"Well, she was just here."

Betsey said, "Bernard, are you funning me?"

"No," said Bernard. "You know something else, she bought one painting from me."

Betsey said, "Bernard you are teasing me."

"No. It's true, and you want to know something even stranger, she's coming back tomorrow to take painting lessons."

Betsey said, "Now I know you're lying."

"No, Betsey, I can't believe it myself, except the rose painting is gone and I have eighty pounds in my pocket. You know something else, I have been writing to her and sending her poems, and she doesn't know it's me."

"You sure are in a pickle," said Betsey, laughing.

Bernard said, "Yes, I know, and I have got to watch myself."

"What on Earth caused them to stop here at this old garage?" asked Betsey.

"They told me they had been to a boot sale. They parked near the garage and were on their way back when they saw my paintings. I have never experienced anything this weird in all my life. It is as if it's from another planet," said Bernard.

"I know what you will be doing the rest of the day," said Betsey.

"I know, I've got to get the place cleaned up the best I can," said Bernard.

"You go ahead and get started, and I will bring some rags and cleaning supplies as soon as I finish these beans and help you," Betsey replied.

As best they could, it being an old building, Betsey and Bernard spent the rest of the afternoon cleaning the old garage.

Bernard said, "We are eating at the pub tonight, Betsey."

She said, "I'll take you up on that, because I'm too tired to cook tonight."

After getting back from the pub, Bernard saw Lilly's CDs and the stationery he had been writing to her with. He put the stationery on top of the kitchen cabinet and the CDs in his dresser drawer, leaving only one out so she would not suspect anything.

Before Lilly started painting, Bernard thought he might slip up and Lilly would find out he was Art and the one sending those letters. After putting some thought into the situation, he decided to write one more letter to correct the matter and to keep her from being suspicious. He wrote to her and explained that because of his work he would not be writing for some time, and then he mailed the letter.

Bernard had a fretful night, tossing and turning, thinking of Lilly coming to paint. He got up early in anticipation of Lilly coming to take painting lessons. He had his coffee and munched on some toast and jelly so as not to mess up the kitchen. He washed the cup and tableware that he used to keep the area clean, and he put them away. He made a quick trip to the grocery and bought a variety of sliced meats, cheese, chicken, and ham salad to make sure there was enough food. He did not want to be embarrassed by not having enough food to eat.

Bernard laid out the paints and brushes that they would need to paint. He took a sharp kitchen knife into the flower garden and cut some flowers, then put them in an old fruit jar that Betsey had sitting on the shelf. He filled the jar half full of water and set it in the middle of the kitchen table. He put on some easy listening music and turned on the CD player so Lilly could hear the music when she came. He sat down in anticipation, thinking she would not show up for lessons because she was so busy in the music business. He was still thinking it must be a dream, except the rose painting was missing from the window shelf and he had an extra eighty pounds in his pocket.

Bernard stayed in the back, not wanting to show how anxious he was. At 9:50, he heard the door open and the bells jingling on the front door.

"Hello," said Lilly.

Bernard's heart began to increase its rhythm. "Hello," replied Bernard, "come on back."

Lilly appeared around the corner of the door facing. Bernard looked up, and there stood the prettiest woman in the world as far as Bernard was concerned. She was dressed in a yellow peasant blouse and a full-length tan skirt with slit pockets and brown flat shoes, with a huge smile on her face.

Bernard was all smiles from ear to ear. Bernard said, "When you came in, it was like golden sunshine lit up the place." Bernard was all thumbs; he was so nervous getting an apron for her to keep paint off her clothes. He let her put on the apron, but he tied it for her in the back.

He started off calling her Ms. Lilly; she stopped him by saying, "My name is just Lilly. I was raised on a sheep farm and I am as common as they get. Walking through sheep manure makes a person humble and puts you in your place. So, we will call each other by our first names, okay?"

Bernard smiled and said "Sure, but I will feel out of place." Bernard asked her to sit in his chair at the easel next to the small table with the paints he had already laid out. He pulled up another chair next to her. He was thinking to himself it was hard to believe he was sitting next to a famous singer he thought was the best in the world.

Lilly, seeing the fresh cut flowers and hearing the music, teased Bernard, "This seems like a first date rather than a painting lesson. I appreciate it when people do nice things for me when they don't have to," She looked at Bernard as his face turned red.

Bernard, trying to change the subject, said, "I have taped butcher paper over the canvas to practice on. Then, when we start to paint, we will use the canvas. The first thing we will do is practice making leaves of all kinds, then switch to making petals, then to painting flowers. I will tape your practice papers to the wall so you can see your progress."

He showed her how to prepare her brush with a mix of paint thinner and linseed oil. Bernard illustrated how the leaf was painted, then had her do the same. As she began to make progress, he asked, "Why didn't your friend come along?"

Lilly said, "Mary, the woman who was with me yesterday?"

"Yes," said Bernard.

"She is my cousin. She handles all my books and accounts. She has a full-time job keeping up with my business."

Lilly was making good progress with the leaves, so Bernard showed her how to make another type, then on to another type. Bernard told her she was doing great, which made her smile and feel happy as a child when they achieve something for the first time. People are always overjoyed when they accomplish something of an artistic endeavor for the first time.

They switched back and forth on different leaves. She was beginning to get good at this, so he told her it was time to make flower petals. He outlined some petals and made marks for her to follow. He blocked in the first one, then began to demonstrate making petals. He gave her the brush and let her try to do as he did. She did well on blocking in the petals, but when Bernard showed her how to put the highlights on the petals, she was having difficulties. She tried again but was not able to control her strokes. Bernard stood up and said, "Hold your brush as you normally hold it, and I will hold your hand and guide you through the brush stroke and make the flip of the brush at the end of the stroke."

Putting his hand on the back of the chair to keep from becoming unbalanced, and he put his right hand over her hand, holding the brush to control the brush stroke. Then there was trouble right here in the middle of the little green garage. He smelled her perfume and her hair odor and could hardly control his right hand to show her the flip.

Trying to control himself while lingering long enough to take in that wonderful aroma, he was able to follow through with the stroke. He moved back and sat in his chair to put some distance between them.

To Lilly, it felt good to have a strong man's hand to guide her. She turned to Bernard and smiled at him, thinking he was not bad-looking either. He had deep-set hazel eyes, a square jaw, a full head of salt-and-pepper hair, nice lips, and heavy eyebrows that framed his face. Yes, she could be comfortable with a man like that, only a little younger. After practicing for about two hours, it was getting close to noon, and Lilly was making good progress making leaves and petals.

Bernard suggested they take a break for lunch. "What do we do for lunch?" asked Lilly.

Bernard said, "I have taken care of that. I have ham, cheese, and crackers, chicken salad and ham salad, apples, and crisps, as you call them. I have wine, fizz water, and Cokes."

"Wine sounds good," said Lilly, "but I will have fizz water. Do you have a lemon?"

"Yes," said Bernard.

She helped gather the food, and Bernard said, "The weather is nice, so we will sit outside on the café chairs and table."

"Oh, we will have a picnic," replied Lilly.

"Somewhat," said Bernard, handing her a cloth to spread on the table. They both carried the food to the table. Bernard brought out the chair pads that Betsey had stored away in the garage, to keep Lilly from having to sit on the hard iron chairs.

The table was partially shaded, which made for a more comfortable outing. As they were eating, Lilly asked

Bernard how he found the place. Bernard explained how he was looking for a place to rent and just walking down the street when he saw the flowers through the hedge fence. He told her he did not intend to stay long, because he was just passing through to Europe. But upon finding that the garage was for rent, and with the flower garden, he had all the subject matter he needed.

"Look around you, Lilly, with all the blooming flowers and shrubs, this place is a paradise, and it sits right in the outskirts of London. All the people whizzing by do not have any idea this place exists. The Japanese are experts at taking small places like this and making them a work of art. They make them appear larger than they really are, the way they design them. Betsey has done a wonderful job making this place beautiful, and she even has a koi pond up by the house. People do not slow down and enjoy the world they live in."

Bernard told Lilly, "Look at the bees collecting pollen and how well organized they are. Small insects look after each other and work together for the benefit of all. They have more intellect and compassion in that small brain than humans. In humanity, we chase after things of monetary value, and in doing so we trample the sick and poor and underprivileged into the dirt, not caring what they do. Whether a sick person lives or dies depends on how much profit someone will make."

Lilly began looking at Bernard and saw him for the first time. Here was a man comfortable with his surroundings, not ashamed to live in an old, converted garage. He sees the world differently than other men, a man who, unashamed, paints flowers for their beauty and color. He sees beyond what the common person sees. He encapsulates more wisdom than the common person. He is not a bad-looking guy, with the gray-blue deep-set eyes that look like a wild animal on the prowl looking for prey. If he were younger, I would be willing to be his prey but, he is too old. However, he is someone who grows on you.

As Bernard spoke, it jarred Lilly out of her daydream. Bernard said, "It is time to get back to work. In this solitude, a person could spend the whole day out here."

They cleared the table and put away the food, then got back to the easel. Bernard said, "I want you to paint a large single flower and some smaller ones with a mixture of different leaves. This time we will paint on canvas."

Lilly replied, "Oh, it is too soon."

"It is okay," said Bernard, "I will guide you through it." Bernard made an outline of the large flower with his brush in burnt sienna, then outlined the small flowers and leaves. After outlining, he showed her how to lay in color around the perimeter using blue, mauve, and yellow, then work light gray into them. He had her make the leaves, correcting her as needed, then had her block in the large flower in the manner he had shown her.

Lilly asked Bernard why he came to England. He replied he and his wife had made a tour of Europe and he was retracing that journey after his wife died of cancer, only this time he was going to take as long as he wanted and paint if he wished.

"I am sorry to hear that about your wife," said Lilly.

Bernard continued to correct her strokes until the large flower was completed. Then he showed her how to make the small flowers.

"How long are you staying here in London?" asked Lilly.

Bernard looked at her and smiled, then said, "As long as you want me to teach you."

Lilly grinned and flushed red in the face. "Where did you say you were from?" asked Lilly.

"I am from Tennessee, and I live in Nashville, but I was born in Monterey, Tennessee," he answered.

"Nashville—isn't that what is called Music City?"

"Yes, but the only music I hear is the jingle of my tax money going into the city coffers to support bars and hotels downtown!"

Lilly laughed.

"Now, put some small leaves here and here," said Bernard, outlining the area for her.

Lilly, looking at her watch, said, "It is almost 2:30 and time for me to go."

"You may stay as long as you like. We need to finish your painting."

After they finished the painting, Bernard said, "Let's sit outside for a while. Painting tires a person out."- Lilly went outside, and Bernard took the CD player and extension cord outside and set it on an old wooden motor oil crate. They sat at the little café table and listened to the soft music.

Lilly was on cloud nine learning to paint. such a beautiful garden, she thought, and Bernard is not too shabby either. Lilly, looking at the garden of flowers and enjoying the view, said, "I see what you mean, a paradise."

Bernard said, "Betsey, the lady I rent the garage from, has a little fox that watches for her when she gardens. The fox comes near, waiting for her to scare a mouse or grasshopper out, then catches it."

Just then, Betsey came up and asked Bernard if he would take her buckets of water to the back of the garden so she could water some baskets that were hanging on the fence.

"Sure," replied Bernard. He introduced Betsey to Lilly, saying she was his new student. Betsey said she was glad to meet her and had heard of her.

As he was going to get the buckets, Betsey yelled for him to just take one at a time as they were too heavy. Bernard came back with both buckets filled to the brim. Betsey admonished him that he was going to hurt his back. As Bernard passed, he said, "This saves me a trip."

When he was out of hearing distance, Betsey, still watching him, told Lilly, "That man is as strong as an ox. He is carrying over ninety pounds as though it was nothing to him. He moved some heavy furniture for me as though it was nothing. It's a lucky woman who snags that man. He will do anything I ask him. He drops his brush and comes running."

Bernard came back from water duty. Betsey thanked him and proceeded to walk to the back of the garden. Lilly asked Bernard how he liked his landlady. Bernard, watching Betsey watering her plants, said, "She's not a landlady, she is family. She will do anything for you. She has a heart of gold. Sometimes, she cooks extra food and brings it to me."

Lilly liked the simplicity of the place. Finally she said, "I must go. May I take my painting with me? I would like to show it to Mary."

"Sure," said Bernard.

They went back into the building, and Lilly looked at her finished painting. Looking at Bernard, she asked, "what do you think?"

Bernard replied, "Very good for your first time, and better than most."

That brought a big smile to Lilly's face. She asked, "Do I pay you now or at the end of the week?"

"At the end of the week," he replied. "As famous as you are, I should be paying you," he said with a smile on his face.

Lilly started to laugh but bit the side of her lip to keep from laughing. She said, "I will bring sandwiches tomorrow. Which do you like, tuna or egg salad?"

"Either one," said Bernard.

"Okay, I will bring both," she replied. "We'll each take half of each one."

Bernard took her painting to the car and placed it on paper so it would not fall over. Lilly was overjoyed and gave Bernard a big hug, and she said she would see him tomorrow.

Bernard watched her drive away in her powder-blue Jaguar. Bernard was thinking that he might never have her for his own, but he got to spend time with her now.

Bernard went over to Betsey's house and invited her to go to the pub with him for supper. She was glad to accept, having worked in the garden most of the day. While in the pub eating, Bernard filled her in on how the class went that day.

Betsey said, "You must think you are in heaven."

Bernard just smiled.

On arriving back home, Lilly could not wait to show

Mary what she had painted. Mary thought it was great for her first time, and she asked Lilly how the day went.

Lilly, thinking to herself and grinning at how the day went, said "Oh, okay."

Mary repeated, "Lilly, I see you hiding that smile on your face. I asked, how did the day go?"

Lilly, still smiling, said, "He is wonderful. I have never met anyone like him. He is so aware of his surroundings, more so than most people. He is aware of things that other people take for granted." Hesitating, she said, "I wish he was my age."

Mary said, "What has age got to do with it?"

Lilly replied, "He's too old."

Mary said, "Well, your two husbands and the rest of your boyfriends were your age. How did that turn out?"

Bernard lay awake that night trying to get some sleep, still in disbelief at how this all came about, but knowing nothing would become of it. There was just too much difference in their age. However, Bernard was looking forward to the next day's class, and he was glad to be spending time with Lilly. It would be any man's dream to be able to spend time with her.

Lilly was up earlier than normal the next morning to make tuna and egg salad sandwiches. Mary came in, grinning. Teasing Lilly, she said, "Well, I see you are already preparing his meals for him."

Lilly said, "Mind your own business," with a grin on her face. Finishing the sandwiches, she went back to her dressing room to check her hair and make-up. She picked up the sandwiches and was on her way out the door to the little green garage.

Bernard was also up early, having tossed and turned most of the night. Hurrying through breakfast, he went outside to cut fresh flowers for the table where they would paint. After making sure the area was clean, he laid out a new clean palette of colors for Lilly to use. Making sure the brushes were clean, he started the music on the CD player.

Finally, Lilly arrived, and she was earlier today than yesterday. She was as excited to get back to painting as Bernard was to have her. She brought the sandwiches and asked Bernard to put them in the refrigerator, which Bernard was happy to do.

Bernard turned to Lilly and said, "My, you look fresh and pretty. This place just lights up when you walk in just like a ray of sunshine." Lilly bit her lip to keep from smiling too much. Bernard asked Lilly, "Are you ready to start a new day?"

"Yes," she replied, "I could not wait to be back."

Bernard instructed her to start back on the leaves and petals to refresh her skills and memory. Lilly, standing at the easel, started practicing painting leaves. Later, he had her switch over to painting flower petals.

As time wore on, Bernard told Lilly, "I've noticed you don't have a wedding ring on. Are you not married?"

"No," said Lilly.

"Boyfriend?" asked Bernard.

"No," Lilly replied.

"My goodness, such a beautiful woman as you, and the sweetest personality—I thought men would be dropping at your feet."

Lilly now had stopped painting and was just dabbing the paint on the palette and stirring the paint with her brush in a reminiscing thought. Lilly said, "No, my boyfriend and I just broke up. I just do not seem to be able to connect with the right men. I have been married twice. My first husband could not leave the women alone while I was on tour. My second husband was robbing me blind. I don't know what is wrong with me."

Bernard saw a tear running down Lilly's face. Alarmed and saddened that he had brought the subject up, he grabbed some tissue from the box on the table. Putting his arm around Lilly's back, he dabbed her tears and said, "Here, here Lilly, this is a happy place, not a sad one."

Lilly, looking up at Bernard and into his eyes, saw a humble and caring man, a sight she was not used to. Lilly started to smile and tried to laugh.

Bernard, releasing Lilly, said, "I am so sorry, I shouldn't have asked. I thought with your beauty and personality, you would have men falling all over you. I am startled in disbelief. I am so sorry."

Lilly, wiping her nose and still looking at Bernard, said, "Apparently you care more about me than they did." She stared into his face.

Bernard, thoughtfully wishing he was younger, said, "Let's take a break to refresh ourselves. I will pour each of us a glass of wine."

Bernard poured each of them a half glass of wine and said, "Let's sit outside at the café table." Sitting at the table, Bernard pointed at the flower garden and said, "See Lilly, this is our own little world right here. Every morning when I get up and come out here in the fresh air, looking over the flower garden, I see a new day and a new beginning. Here we are able to shuck off our unhappiness and leave our troubles behind."

Lilly asked, "Bernard, how do you know if someone really loves you?"

Bernard replied, "If a person really loves you, he will put you first in his life. True love and devotion are not a contest. It is a committed partnership. I have never felt the need to run with the boys. I did not find the need to join a club. I wanted to be with and be totally committed to the one I love. The point is, you should live for each other. Everyone else and every other thing are side issues."

Lilly was more and more gaining insight into Bernard's life. He was a different type of man that she has seen before, truly a man comfortable with himself. She started feeling good being there with Bernard and his insights on life. Whenever Bernard was busy and not looking, Lilly watched his every movement. After they finished their wine, Bernard said, "It's time to get back to work."

Lilly, feeling better, started back to painting flower petals. Bernard told her to paint the petals from the outside inwards, following the contours of the petal.

Lilly replied, "This is not as easy as it looks."

Bernard told her, "A person's brain tries to make him do the opposite of what he should do. This is why some people give up." After about forty-five minutes of this, Bernard said, "It's time to break for lunch."

Bernard retrieved the sandwiches from the refrigerator as Lilly laid the cloth on the café table. They gathered their condiments and crisps. Lilly separated the sandwiches and gave Bernard half of the egg salad sandwich and half of the tuna salad one. While they were eating, Bernard said "This is as good as it gets. It is our own little Garden of Eden."

Lilly said, "Yes, this is the best part of my day."

Bernard looked and smiled at her and said, "Anytime you are here is my best part of my day."

Lilly grinned and said, "I sure enjoy it here. How is your sandwich?"

"Very good! It is exceptional. I do not believe I have ever had a better one. I appreciate them. Thanks for bringing them. A woman's touch is always better than a man's."

Lilly laughed but appreciated his thoughtfulness.

After eating lunch and enjoying each other's company, they got back to painting. They cleared the café table and put the extra food back in the refrigerator.

Bernard prepared a canvas for her by blocking off the sections of canvas for the different flowers. With him guiding her through the process, finally she finished the painting. Lilly was overjoyed, and Bernard bragged on her endeavor.

They took another break and sat outside for a while, listening to the music. After a while, Lilly told Bernard it was time to go, as much as she hated to. They went back inside, and Bernard bragged on her painting. Bernard carried her painting to the car and placed it so it would not move. Lilly gave Bernard a big hug and said she would bring sandwiches again tomorrow. Bernard waited and watched as she drove out of sight in the blue Jaguar.

Arriving back at her condominium, Lilly carried in her painting of multiple flower groups and showed the painting to Mary. Mary told her it was very pretty. Lilly settled in on the couch drawing her feet up under her, as Mary began to question her on how her day went.

With a big smile, Lilly started telling Mary all about

Bernard and how he painted, things he said and thought. In doing this, Lilly picked up a throw pillow beside her and absentmindedly wrapped her arms around it.

Mary noticed Lilly hugging the pillow while talking about Bernard. The more she talked about Bernard, the tighter she hugged the pillow. Mary asked Lilly, "What are you doing?"

Lilly said, "Nothing, just talking to you. Why?"

Mary, smiling said, "What are you doing with the pillow?"

Lilly then noticed she was hugging the pillow. Turning red in the face and blushing, she said, "Oh!" and threw the pillow at Mary. Mary, catching the pillow, laughed.

Lilly said, "He is too old for me, though."

Mary said, "That is probably what he thinks also. He's certainly a cut above the rest of the men in your life."

Lilly said, "It is getting almost time to go out and eat. I want to pick up some things for Bernard's lunch tomorrow."

Mary, teasing Lilly, said, "So now you are making his meals for him?"

Lilly laughed and told Mary to mind her own business as they went out the door.

The next morning, Bernard was up and dusting and sweeping to make things right for Lilly. Bernard had decided to stay here to paint and relax, but now everything revolved around Lilly.

After a while, Lilly came in carrying sandwiches. Bernard looked and said, "Here comes my sunshine," with a big smile. "Hush," said Lilly, "you are embarrassing me."

Bernard, looking at Lilly, said, "You will always be my sunshine because you always radiate such beauty by your presence."

Lilly, changing the subject, asked Bernard to put the sandwiches away in the refrigerator. Then she said, "What are we painting today?"

"I thought we would do an iris today. We can do a purple iris or a yellow one, whichever you would like," said Bernard.

"Let us do a purple one. I haven't used that color."

Bernard laid out the colors she would need and marked off the area for the iris and leaves. He told her to make a light background of yellow ocher and sienna and work in some gray.

As they started painting, Lilly asked Bernard, "What was it like where you grew up?"

Bernard said, "It is a small town in Tennessee on the Cumberland Plateau called Monterey. The town evolved on the sides of an old buffalo and Indian trail. It was the only way to get up or down the edge of plateau, because it is surrounded by cliffs. President Andrew Jackson used this trail to go from Nashville to Washington by stagecoach. A few pioneers settled there, and coal was discovered which in turn brought the railroad. The air was so good, they built two hospitals there for the people who had T.B. Tourists started coming, and there were five hotels built. Finally, there were five coal mines in the plateau area, with a shirt factory, a hardwood flooring company, and several lumber mills. All the hotels burned except one. Then the mines closed, along with the shirt factory and sawmills. The town imploded upon itself. The only way to get a job was to go to college, work in a coal mine, or join the military. I joined the military; that is how I met my wife.

"Growing up was tough. We lived on a forty-acre farm—you might say a one-mule farm—and that is how we kept food on the table. You started doing your share of work at about age five or six. In the spring, after school in the evening, we planted our crops and worked them in the summer all day. In the fall, after school was out, we spent the rest of the day digging and gathering crops. We worked while our friends played. I popped popcorn at the movie to be able to see the movie free."

Bernard told Lilly to paint the contours on the iris to make it look right. After painting for two hours, Bernard said, "It's time for lunch." Lilly laid the cloth and Bernard brought out the food. While they were eating Bernard asked Lilly, "What was it like growing up in England?"

Lilly said, she, her mother, and father lived in London, but her father was in the military and he was killed in the Korean War. "It was too hard on my mother to take care of me and work too. So she sent me to live with her parents when I was six years old. My grandparents were getting old, and Mother's sister and her husband lived there with their daughter, Mary. They took care of the sheep ranch. That is where Mary comes in; she is one year older than me.

"We went to school and church together. We also got in trouble together. When they were shearing sheep, Mary and I would jump on the piles of wool and scatter it everywhere, and grandpa would get after us with a stick, and we would run off screaming. He would laugh, and he would never lay a hand on us.

"One night in the spring, we took a newborn lamb into our room and hid it. Gramps heard it crying and made us take it back to its mother. We played in the creeks and anything that was adventurous. We started singing in the church choir, and I entered a few contests, and here I am.

"Mary went on to college and got a degree in accounting, and I followed a singing career. My second husband nearly stole all my money gambling. That is when I had Mary to take over all my affairs except bookings that are handled by my booking agent."

Bernard said, "You have had an interesting life."

Lilly said, "Yes, but I wish some of it had not been so interesting."

Bernard noticed tears forming in her eyes, and, being alarmed, got his handkerchief. Putting an arm around her back and blotting her tears, he said, "Lilly, I seem to be a harbinger of sad times."

Lilly looked into his eyes and wished she could meld into his arms, but that age difference kept coming up. "It has nothing to do with you, because I look forward being with you. It is the best part of my day," said Lilly. "Through no fault of my own, I keep tripping over my past."

"Well, it is time to get back to work," said Bernard. They cleared the table and put everything away.

Bernard guided her through the painting, and she finished it by the time of the last break. Bernard said, "Let's take a break, and we will check out the painting after our break." Bernard got the drinks and took them to the table.

Lilly sat down, and Bernard took a knife and went into the flower garden and cut several varieties of flowers. Lilly was wondering what he was up to, since he had cut fresh flowers in the morning. Bernard returned with a large bunch of flowers, placed them in Lilly's arms, and said, "I'll be right back." He got his camera and proceeded to take several pictures of Lilly holding the flowers.

Putting his camera on the table, he took the flowers from Lilly and said, "I will put them in water, and you can take them home with you when you go." He told Lilly, "Of all the flowers in your arms, you are the prettiest of them all."

He put the flowers in a vase and came back and sat down with Lilly. After talking for a while, Bernard said, "It is time to check your painting."

They went back into the building and checked the painting for improvements to be corrected and defects to make right. After a few touch-ups, Bernard said, "I think you have a winner."

Lilly was beaming with pride and had a big smile on her face as she looked at the finished painting. Then she looked at Bernard, thinking of what a good person he was to take time out from his trip to teach her when he did not have to. He looked after Betsey and helped her, also, taking her to the pub and buying her supper. Lilly was thinking about the men in her past who only thought of themselves. Here is a man at the start of his vacation, she thought, taking time out to help others. He certainly was not cut from the same cloth as the other men in her life were. Lilly was more and more getting attached to this new man in her life.

Bernard said, "Let's sit outside until it's time for you to go."

He asked Lilly what she wanted to drink.She said, "Fizz water, lemon, please."

Bernard collected the drinks, took them outside, and sat

them on the table. He went back in and brought out the CD player, then sat it on a wooden oilcan box and started playing good listening music.

Lilly asked Bernard what the secret was of being a good painter.

Bernard said, "There is a secret, but it's the same with all artistic endeavors, and the same secret you use in singing. It is called practice, practice, practice. It is the same with musicians. A famous guitar player in Nashville said that when he went to the bathroom, he took his guitar with him because he did not want to lose any time practicing. He was one of the foremost guitar players in the world."

Bernard told her, "You are doing very well for a beginner. I am proud of the progress you have made in this short time."

After a while, Lilly told Bernard it was time to go. She hated to leave, but he needed to rest.

Bernard said, "Not at all. When you are here, I always feel refreshed." Lilly smiled.

Bernard went inside and got the flowers out of the vase and wrapped them in damp newspaper, then in plastic to keep water from dripping on her car. She took her painting, and he took the flowers and placed them in the car. He placed the painting where it could not move.

Lilly reached out and gave Bernard a friendly hug because she was so happy with the painting. Bernard, of course, returned the hug. But then something happened. Lilly hesitated.For some reason, she did not want to let go. Then, releasing Bernard, she looked up sheepishly and turned red in the face. Trying to grin, she told Bernard she would see him tomorrow and would bring the sandwiches. Lilly got into the powder-blue Jaguar sedan and waved to Bernard, then drove away. Still embarrassed, she hoped Bernard did not think too much about it.

Bernard did not think too much about it because it is only normal for people to react that way when they do something extraordinary as creating a painting. It gives you a feeling of euphoria. You have created something out of nothing through your mind and skill. Bernard was determined to stay at arm's length because of his age and the possibility of her thinking him a fool.

Bernard took his film and got it developed to paint Lilly's portrait. He had extra copies of photos made for Lilly.

Returning home, Lilly could not wait to show Mary what she had painted. Mary thought it was great. She had Mary retrieve the flowers and put them in a vase.

When Mary returned, she saw Lilly staring at the painting with a blank look on her face. Mary, seeing Lilly's mind was far away, said, "What happened today?"

Lilly coming to her senses, said, "Nothing," trying to hide her feelings.

Mary said, "Something is bothering you; what is it?"

Lilly said, "Today I was telling him about my past, and I got tearful. He put his arm around my back, and I wanted to meld into his arms. When I was leaving, I hugged him as I always do, and I was.so elated by the flowers and the painting that when I hugged Bernard, I was so happy, I ..." She stopped talking, tears forming in her eyes, looking at the painting.

Mary, waiting for an answer, said, "So?"

Lilly looked at Mary and said through teary eyes, "I didn't want to let go."

"Well, why did you?" asked Mary.

Lilly replied, "Oh, he's too old. I wish he was my age."

Mary said, "What's age got to do with it?"

Lilly replied, "What will people think?"

Mary said, "The people who matter will think you are in love and happy. Who cares what the others will think? Lilly, your love life has been in turmoil all your life. Here is someone who really cares for you, unlike the other men in your life that you have been with. You could have twenty or thirty years with Bernard; that's more than you have now. How old is he?" "He is forty-eight."

"And you?"

"Thirty-one."

Mary said, "That is seventeen years. So, you had twelve years of hell. Now you have a chance of thirty or more years of bliss. How does that add up in your book? Lilly, you need to think long and hard about this man. It may be your last chance for real happiness."

Lilly did not sleep well. Arthur was writing love letters, and now someone else was stealing her heart.

The next morning Lilly was up early and in the kitchen preparing food for her and Bernard. This time she baked a lemon pie. She got herself made up and in a nice dress.

Mary came in and saw Lilly preparing food and said, "Are you going to paint or going on a date?"

"I don't need any of your sarcasm," said Lilly, smiling.

Mary looking Lilly in the eyes and said, "Lilly, let yourself go and quit holding back. I have never seen you this happy."

Lilly, looking sheepish said, "Help me put this in the car." Then Lilly drove off toward the little green garage.

Bernard heard the bells jingling in the front and came around the corner of the doorway to see Lilly carrying the food. Bernard was astonished at how beautiful Lilly looked. "Wow!" said Bernard, "if you get any more beautiful, I won't be able to hold my composure to teach."

Lilly smiled at the compliment and asked Bernard to get the pie out of the car.

After retrieving the pie, Bernard said, "Lilly, I don't know what to say. I knew you were pretty, but now, wow! When you go outside in the flower garden, all the flowers will look dull compared to you."

Lilly was beaming at his compliment. She was becoming more and more attached to Bernard.

A few days after Lilly began painting, another tan envelope arrived at Lilly's condominium while she was taking art lessons. Mary saved the letter until Lilly arrived home. That afternoon, after seeing Lilly's artwork, Mary told her that a letter had come. This put Lilly in a happy mood. She hurriedly opened the envelope and began to read:

Dear Lilly,

My work will not allow me to write to you for a while. I hope you will understand.

Lilly was saddened about this information, and tears filled her eyes as she continued to read. She looked forward to his letters.

I wrote you another poem and send my love to you. It is called "Beauty and Grace."

A TOUCH OF MAUVE

Beauty and Grace
Your face is like a beautiful flower when it blooms
Your beauty and brightness light up every room
When I first saw you take a look at me
Such radiance and beauty was all I could see
When I first saw you as you looked my way
You disarmed me and I did not know what to say
I wished to take you into my loving arms
To embrace you and absorb your many charms
When you said hello your voice echoed in my brain
One look at such beauty could drive a man insane
When you had to leave and go your merry way
The room grew dark and turned to gray
As now both our lives are incomplete
I long for the day when again we shall meet.

I am looking for a brighter future.
Love,
Art

Lilly's eyes began to glisten with tears as she knew she would not be hearing from Art for a while. However, she now had Bernard for companionship. She wondered what type of work he did that would take him away from writing to her.

Lilly showed the letter to Mary, and Mary said, "Such a sweet poem." Mary, looking closer at the poem, asked Lilly, "Where have you been lately? He says 'until we meet again.' I know it is just a poem, but he writes as if he has met you."

Lilly reread the poem and said, "Nowhere other than usual."

Mary asked Lilly, "What is Bernard's other given name?"

Lilly said, "I have no idea."

Mary said, "Ask him tomorrow, and if his name is not Arthur, at least that would eliminate him."

Lilly took the letter and placed it in her purse with the other letters.

Chapter 3

Lilly and Mary decided to take a Saturday break and go to a flea market/boot sale. They dressed casually but wore large, brimmed hats and oversized sunglasses so Lilly would not be recognized. They enjoyed mixing with people, but wanted to be left to themselves.

They, for the fun of it, enjoyed refreshments while walking around. They bought a few cute figurines to go with Lilly's collections, as they were not in need of anything. They finally grew tired and decided to leave.

As they were driving back to their condominium, on the way they passed a large sign in a yard which read "Clairvoyant—Read your past and future." Lilly, thinking about the letters she had in her purse, told Mary to turn around. "Go back; I want to see that clairvoyant. I would like to see if she can tell me anything about these letters from Art."

Mary said, "You don't believe in that junk, do you?"

"Not really," said Lilly, "but it won't hurt to try. It would be good entertainment." They both laughed.

When Mary got to a place where she could turn the car around, they headed back to the house that had the sign in the yard. They parked the car and went up to the house. A sign on the door said, "Open, Come In." They went inside to what used to be a living room, with a large desk and several chairs. A sign on the desk said to ring a bell for service.

Lilly rang the bell. In a few minutes, an older lady came into the room from the back of the house.

The lady greeted them and asked how she could help them. Lilly said, "I have some letters. I would like to see if you can tell me anything about them and who wrote them." The lady said, "Sometimes I can get a reading, and sometimes I can't. I am not a fortune teller. I have observations of some things, and sometimes I do not. However, the cost is the same. I charge fifty pounds for the first reading whether or not I can decipher anything. If I do, and if you want a second reading, the cost is twenty-five pounds, but I cannot guarantee anything."

Lilly said, "That is all right; I would like to try."

The lady invited them into the next room that used to be a dining room, with a large and very heavy table and chairs with a buffet against the wall opposite two windows, decorated with heavy curtains and a chandelier over the table. There was seating for six people. The lady took a seat at the end of the table farther from the door, Lilly took a seat to the lady's right, and Mary sat next to Lilly. The lady told Lilly that it would be fifty pounds in cash before she started. Lilly reached into her purse and counted out fifty pound notes and gave them to the lady. The lady put the money aside and asked for the letters. Lilly reached into her purse and pulled out the letters, which were wrapped neatly with a white ribbon tied in a bow. She then handed them to the clairvoyant.

The clairvoyant asked Lilly what she wanted to know.

Lilly said, "Anything that you can tell me about the person that wrote them, I would appreciate it."

The lady asked that they not talk, as this would interrupt her concentration. The clairvoyant rubbed her fingers over the letters, opening and closing her eyes from time to time. She then looked at Lilly and said, "You tell me about him. I get a vision of him holding your hand."

Lilly looked at Mary with dismay. She was at a loss for who it could be.

The lady then said, "I see dark clouds hanging over your past. You have had a disappointing love life, haven't you?"

Lilly said, "Yes," then looked at Mary with a puzzled look on her face.

The clairvoyant said, "This man is different. I do not know who he is—that does not come through to me—but you do know him. Everything I tell you is symbolic. I only get images, then I try to interpret them for you. As I see in your past, the men in your life were very flamboyant; they came and swept you off your feet. They were like pretty packages wrapped in beautiful, colorful paper tied up in a beautiful ribbon, but when you take off the ribbons and unwrap the paper and look into the box, the box is empty. There is nothing in there for you but anguish and dust. The man who wrote these letters is different. He is as plain as an old cardboard box tied with a string. When you take off the string and open the box, the box is filled with jewels of all kinds. It is filled with gold, silver, diamonds, pearls, rubies, and emeralds. These are all symbolic; they stand for his character. The pearls stand for pearls of wisdom. His loyalty is golden and unwavering. He is giving, caring, compassionate, and committed. I see that this man is deeply in love with you. I see the color mauve surrounding him. The only thing that I can tell you is this mystery will be revealed by the color mauve."

Lilly asked if she could be more specific.

"I can only tell you this color is very strong around him. It could be a room or a shirt, or maybe he just likes mauve. One thing is for sure, you will know without a doubt when he and this color come together. I must give you a warning. There is a shadow hanging over this situation, and I do not know what this shadow is, but you will have only one chance to make this come about. If you do, you are in for the ride of your life. I see a union clasped in iron, never to come apart." The clairvoyant ended the session, saying, "There is a reason he has not revealed himself to you, but I don't know what that reason is. That is all I can tell you. You can come back later, and I might be able to tell you more, but I cannot promise." She handed the letters back to Lilly.

Lilly and Mary got up and thanked the clairvoyant for the reading. While leaving the building on the way to the car, Lilly asked Mary, "What do you make of that?" Mary said, "I do not know, but it looks as though you have a man in your future." Then she said, "She sure knew a lot about your past."

Lilly said, "That is scary. I do not know anyone like she described. She said he has held my hand, which is more of a puzzle." As they were riding back to the condominium, they kept trying to figure out who it might be. While trying out the possibilities of finding out and solving this mystery, Lilly said, "I have not been around any men except James, and we can forget that."

"What about Bernard?" said Mary.

Lilly said "No, I don't think he is the romantic type; he is more the practical type. Besides, I do not think he is interested in me. He only has one of my recordings. He also is too old for me."

Mary said, "Lilly, that is going to come back to haunt you someday."

Monday morning Lilly got up early and prepared two sandwiches for her and Bernard, along with some fruit. Mary came in while Lilly was preparing and said, "Well, you are still cooking for your man. You never did that for the other men in your life."

"Well, the other men in my life didn't appreciate what I did for them." Lilly laughed and said, "Mind your own business, okay? You know he is too old for me."

"Don't knock it; he still has blood flowing in his veins," said Mary. They both laughed. "On a cold night, almost any man will do," laughed Mary.

Lilly laughed and threw a piece of celery at Mary, then said, "I have got to get out of here before you have me married."

Mary said, "Lilly, you are always thinking about Art, a relationship that may never evolve, but have you ever stopped to think what it would be like if Bernard went away?"

Lilly stopped cutting the sandwiches, the knife still in her hand, and stared at the blank wall thinking about how she and Bernard enjoyed each other's company, how they seemed to click together, and the happiness he had brought into her life. Lilly dropped the knife on the counter and said, "I wouldn't like it."

Mary walked away, having made her point. Lilly packed her food in the Jaguar and drove off.

On arrival at the little green garage, Lilly was in an uplifted mood and in high spirits. She was always glad to be with Bernard, spending the day laughing and painting. Bernard was waiting to see the lady that lit up the place with her beauty and personality. Bernard always looked forward to Lilly's presence . He told her that when she came with her cheerfulness, it made the room seem to glow.

Lilly put the food in the refrigerator and asked Bernard what they would be painting that day. Bernard replied that they would paint a yellow rose with some mauve flowers to go with the rose, since the colors complement each other. This caught Lilly's attention since the clairvoyant told her the mystery would be revealed with the color mauve.

Lilly went over to the palette and looked at the colors Bernard had laid out and labeled. Lilly said, "The mauve color does not look too impressive; it is very dark."

Bernard said, "Mix a little white into it."

Lilly picked up a little white and mauve with the palette knife and mixed them together, and the color purple exploded into a bright and beautiful color.

"Wow," said Lilly, "I have seen mauve before, but never like that."

Bernard said, "You can make it as light or as dark as you want it."

"How did they come up with this color?" asked Lilly.

Bernard replied, "A young English schoolboy named William Perkin invented it. This was in the days when clothes were not colorfast. His chemistry teacher and other students were trying to make synthetic quinine out of coal tar to treat malaria. William built himself a lab in the upstairs of his house, and he carried on with the experiments. He had gone through twenty-two processes and discovered that color. It was colorfast in wool but not cotton. He kept experimenting until he was able to make cotton colorfast. The rest is history. Women were wearing mauve-colored clothes everywhere. It started a revolution in colorfast dyes."[1]

Bernard marked the outline for the yellow rose, the leaves, and the mauve flowers. He started Lilly laying in some background, then the leaves, then the yellow rose and mauve flowers. After a couple of hours, Bernard suggested they break for lunch and relax outside.

Lilly set the cloth, and Bernard brought the food out with the wine and fizz water for Lilly. Lilly went back in and got her purse and set it beside her while she was eating. As she finished the last sandwich, she reached into her purse and pulled out the parchment letters that Bernard had sent to her, signed "Art." When Bernard saw them, he almost choked on his sandwich. Lilly opened the last one that she had received and read it privately.

Bernard, not knowing what to do, finally asked Lilly "Is that a letter from your boyfriend?"

She replied, "Maybe," without looking up. After reading the letter, she tied the letters back up with the ribbon and put them back in her purse.

---

[1] Source: Simon Garfield, *Mauve: How One Man Invented a Color That Changed the World.* New York: W.W. Norton, 2002.

Bernard thought to himself that he had better watch out or she would discover that it was he who wrote them. In order to find out how Lilly felt about the letters, he asked, "Are those love letters?"

She said, "Yes."

He asked her if she liked him.

She said, "Yes; he is very romantic."

He asked her, "Is he really?"

She answered, "Yes, he writes me poems."

Thinking of what she and Mary had discussed about Arthur's poem, she asked Bernard what his other given name was.

He replied, "Charles. Charles Bernard Anderson. Why?"

She replied, "You had never mentioned it, and I just wondered."

Because of their age difference, Bernard was determined to keep his distance, and he felt if there ever was a love connection between them, it would have to come from Lilly. He did not want to take away her chance with a younger man who could give her many more years of life than he could. Bernard said, "it's time to go back to work." They gathered up the extra food and utensils and put them away.

Bernard had already had her put in the background and leaves. Now it was time to put in the rose, with Bernard giving advice and directions. After about an hour, with the rose in, he said, "It is time for another break."

They took their drinks out and sat in the café chairs enjoying the beauty of the flowers and shrubs. Betsey came by and asked Bernard, if he would move two large bins to the street. She had filled them with rubbish from the garden shed, and they were too heavy for her to move.

Bernard jumped up and said, "Sure," then retrieved the two large bins from the shed and moved them to the street. Betsey told Lilly she hoped Bernard stayed through the summer, because she could only carry small amounts and had to make a lot of trips because of her back.

Betsey asked Lilly how she liked it here painting with Bernard. "Oh, I love it," beamed Lilly. "He sure is a good teacher. I don't think I would have the patience that he has with people."

"He sure is a fine man," said Betsey. "I have never seen another like him. He fits right in, just like a glove. It is a wonder some woman has not snapped him up for herself."

Lilly was taking this all in while watching Bernard finish his chore, thinking if he was more her age, she would snap him up herself.

When Bernard returned, Betsey thanked him and continued to the back of the garden to water her plants.

"Do you do this much?" asked Lilly.

"What?" asked Bernard.

"Help Betsey," said Lilly.

"Well, I never thought about it," said Bernard, "but I guess I do. With me, it is the natural thing to do. Therefore, I do not even think about it. Any human worth his salt would help others in need without being asked. It would be a sad world if we didn't help each other."

Lilly was beginning to see the real Bernard, a compassionate man. It made her want to put her arms around him and give him a big hug. She saw in him a man who forged his way through life without any of its obstacles in his way. He did not need bravado or to be stroked and groomed. He was completely different from the men of her past. Yes, she thought, I can love a man like that with no holding back. It is just that age difference, but that is beginning to be less important.

Bernard said, "Back to work," and put his hand out and helped her out of her chair. As he took her hand, she felt a warm flush course through her body from his touch. She stepped back and bumped into the chair. Bernard asked if she was all right, and she said, "Yes." He looked deeply into her eyes and asked if she would be all right to finish her painting. She assured him would. She was trying to end the conversation.

Back at the easel, Lilly was having trouble with a brushstroke on the mauve flower. Bernard picked up the brush and, with energy, vigorously put in the brushstrokes to show her how. She was amazed that he could do garden chores and, with a swift stroke of the brush, make everything right, like flipping a switch.

Lilly finished her mauve flowers and put finishing touches on the rest of the canvas. Bernard bragged about her painting and made her feel really proud.

She asked Bernard if she could stay a little while longer; she did not want to go home yet.

Bernard was delighted and said, "What do you want to paint?"

Lilly said, "I do not want to paint. I just want to stay outside with you and listen to music and take in all the beautiful flowers."

Bernard asked if she would like a glass of wine, and she replied, no, just fizz water, because she had to drive.

Bernard brought out the drinks and set them on the café table. Bernard suggested they go down to the koi pond, get some of Betsey's stash of fish food, and feed the fish. Lilly thought that would be great. Bernard got a can of fish food off the back porch, handed it to Lilly, and told her to just sprinkle it over the water. Lilly was overjoyed watching the many mixed colored koi swim around and eat the food.

Bernard watched Lilly as she was feeding the fish, excited just like a little girl watching the fish eat and swim around. Bernard said, "We can paint some fish if you like, on canvas."

"Oh, I would love it," replied Lilly.

Betsey came up behind them and asked if they were having fun.

"Oh yes," said Lilly, "do you mind our feeding them?"

"I don't mind," said Betsey. "If you give them too much, they will stop eating. They are not like humans." Betsey said to Lilly, "You had better watch out; that man grows on you."

Lilly turned beet red and looked at Bernard to see his reaction. Bernard looked at her and smiled. Lilly was enjoying spending extra time with the man she was falling in love with, but she was still wrestling with the age difference.

Betsey went on into her house, leaving Bernard and Lilly to play with the fish and telling them to enjoy themselves. They left the pond and walked some of the paths through the vast array of flowers in the flower garden. Bernard was having a hard time keeping his distance from Lilly. He wished he could take her in his arms and hold her. He was seeing Lilly's inner self coming through as she enjoyed the flowers and fish. He was seeing an innocent and caring person. Bernard would pull a flower and explain how to make the brushstrokes for each of the different varieties. As they came out of the garden, Bernard told Lilly to take a seat and he would be back. Bernard returned with the CD player with the speakers and an extension cord. He plugged it in and played some soft music on the player.

He took his seat, and Lilly moved her chair near his, but a little to the rear so she could watch Bernard's every move, pretending she wanted to be able to hear better when they talked. Lilly was beginning to really admire Bernard.

Lilly asked Bernard if he ever had anything happen in his life that he felt he could not get over, because he seemed so calm and confident.

"Yes," replied Bernard.

"What did you do to get over it?" asked Lilly.

Bernard replied, "Burdens are yours to bear alone. You just plow on through them or set them aside, otherwise they will pull you down, and you will give up. Instead of focusing on your burden, turn to the future. There is usually a bright spot out there somewhere. Every morning, I come outside and look over Betsey's flower garden and see the glory that God has created. It sets the tone for the rest of my day. Sometimes you must change directions. You said you cannot meet the right man. Did you stop to think that perhaps you are fishing in the wrong pond? Some ponds have catfish, some trout, and some bass. You need to find out what you want out of life and what kind of man you want, and do your fishing there. Lilly, just listen to the music we are playing. Listen to the birds singing in the trees and shrubs. We are in another world, not in the ugliness out in the hustle and bustle of commerce on the other side of the hedge."

Lilly was taking in what Bernard was saying and drawing closer with her feelings toward Bernard. Thinking back at the turmoil with the men in her past, she saw right in front of her a very stable, good-looking man. After about thirty minutes of talking and listening to music, Lilly said, "It is getting late, so I had better go to get ahead of the rush hour traffic."

Bernard said, "I will help you with your painting." When they went inside, Bernard bragged about her painting, which made her feel proud of her accomplishment. Bernard carried it to the car and placed it so it would not get damaged.

Lilly gave him a hug and said, "I will see you tomorrow." As Lilly drove away, she felt she was leaving a place where she belonged. It was getting harder and harder to leave this place of happiness with Bernard that she had come to enjoy. It seemed strange that she felt more at home in a little run-down green garage than in an expensive condominium.

When Lilly got home, she showed the painting to Mary, and she thought it was great. Mary asked Lilly, "How was your day?"

Lilly thought a minute and said, "Too good."

"What happened?" asked Mary.

Lilly said, "We sat outside for a while and talked. Then when we were to go back inside and paint, he reached for my hand and pulled me up from my chair. I had a warm rush through my body, and I was not expecting that, so I almost knocked a chair over. He grabbed my arms and said 'are you all right,' and he looked into my eyes with those bedroom eyes of his, and I felt he was looking through me to my very soul. I felt completely nude standing there. I guess I will have to avoid eye contact from now on."

Mary said, "Well, I guess he is not too old after all. Lilly, you have had a rough life with men. Do not let this one fly away. He probably thinks he is too old for you. You are going to have to crack open the door a little to leave him an opening to come in. Throw out a tidbit of bait to see if he takes it.

"You have to see his side of the situation. You are a very famous person, and he is just a common person and probably thinks it is laughable that you would be interested in him. That would be unsurmountable to some people.

"You keep hanging on to those letters. They are just a wisp in the wind. Nothing will come of it. Bernard is flesh and blood and better than anyone you have had in the past. He is someone you can snuggle up to on a cold winter's night."

Mary said, "When we start a new venture in life and into the unknown, it is only natural to hold back. We are uncertain whether or not it is the right decision to make. I can tell you are a changed person since you've been painting with Bernard. Is it because of him, or is it because of the art you are undertaking? You can buy a piece of art and hang it on the wall. However, if it is him, you had better make a decision, because he will not be around forever. How long did he say he was going to stay here?"

Lilly answered, "He said he would stay here as long as I wanted to paint."

"Oh, Lilly, don't you see? He is not staying for that pittance you are paying him. He is staying because of you." Mary asked, "Did you find out his full name?"

"Yes," said Lilly, "it is Charles Bernard Anderson."

"Well, we can rule him out as the one writing those letters."

Chapter 4

Lilly got up early to make sandwiches for herself and Bernard. She wanted to make this an extra special day. Mary noticed the extra preparations that Lilly had been making. Mary, teasing Lilly, said, "Wow, are you planning a banquet?"

"Mind your own business," said Lilly, smiling.

"Why don't you take him with you?" said Mary jokingly.

"I would, but he's too old for me," Lilly replied.

"You wouldn't know it by the feast you are making."

"Get out of here," said Lilly, laughing.

Lilly gathered all her preparations together and packed the car. She drove to the little green garage and cheerfully carried some of the food inside.

"Here, let me help you," said Bernard.

Lilly said, "There is a tray of olives and pickles in the back of the car. Would you get them for me?" Bernard hurried and brought the rest of the food inside.

Lilly noticed Bernard had picked fresh flowers from the garden.

Bernard noticed Lilly had on a new outfit. He asked her to stand back, and he admired her. Her make-up was beautifully done, and her hair was perfect.

He told her to come outside, and he took her picture. He told her in the future, when he bragged to others that he knew her, these pictures would be his proof.

She gave him a big smile and said, "I'm not much to brag about."

He told her, "You are going to make it difficult for me to work with you today, as beautiful as you look."

She was beaming with a smile on her face and asked why.

Bernard said, "You look so gorgeous, I won't be able to concentrate or stay away from you."

Lilly laughed and said, "Oh, I think you will manage."

Lilly said, "We had better put the food away." They went back into the building after putting the food away. Lilly asked, "What are we painting today?"

"Let's paint irises," Bernard said. "I love them because they are so frilly and feminine and have beautiful colors. Here, put on the apron to protect your beautiful dress."

Bernard had already put out the colors to save time. Bernard marked off the outline of the irises for her. He had picked some irises from around the edge of the garden. He began to guide her through the process, trying to stay away from the intoxicating perfume she was wearing.

At noon they took a break for lunch. Lilly spread the cloth on the café table. Bernard took the food out and got the wine. Lilly had made chicken and ham salad extraordinary, with nuts and grapes, and all the trimmings.

Lilly was taking in the beautiful view of the flowers in the garden. This would be the last time for a month she would see this place, if ever. While she was thinking of this, she asked Bernard how long he was going to stay here, knowing he had only planned to stay a month originally. Now he had been here over two months.

Bernard looked at her and said, "I will stay here as long as you take lessons from me."

Lilly turned red in the face. She looked at Bernard in a serious way and said, "I do not want you to stay just for me if you have other things you would rather do."

Bernard replied, "There is nothing in this world I would rather do than to stay here and paint with you."

Lilly felt a flush come over her. She was thinking that here was a man willing to put his life on hold and tend to her wishes. Lilly had to turn away lest she become too emotional, and she had to check herself to keep tears from forming in her eyes. She wondered if Arthur was near the man Bernard was.

Bernard said, "You have made me wonderful meals, and I will surely miss you when you're gone." This made Lilly feel good, knowing he had really enjoyed the sandwiches that she had fixed for him each day.

After they had eaten a leisurely lunch and enjoyed each other's company, Bernard said, "Well, it is time to get back to work." Lilly and Bernard put the food away.

Lilly told Bernard that she had made extra sandwiches for him to eat the next day.

Bernard was really touched and looked at Lilly lovingly, knowing she had gone out of her way to do something special for him. He said, "Thanks, I will surely enjoy them and be thinking of you while I am eating them." Bernard had a special feeling for her, knowing that here was a super-rich woman who did not have to do anything, yet she took the time to make him lunch for tomorrow.

Back at the easel, Bernard walked Lilly through the next

phase of the painting and then the final touch up. Lilly stood back and admired her painting. Bernard said, "Lilly, this is the best one yet. By painting every weekday, you have shortened the learning curve and become a better painter than the average student." Lilly was smiling ear to ear, knowing she had done a good job.

Bernard asked her to come and sit outside for a while to let the painting dry a little and allow the paint to set. He got the glasses and wine and carried them to the café table and chairs. He went back in and brought out the CD player and extension cord, hooked it up, put it on the old oilcan crate, and started playing soft music. Bernard started asking Lilly what her future was going to be like after her tour.

Lilly was noncommittal, saying that the only thing in life she had was to sing, and now, thanks to Bernard, also to paint.

Bernard asked her if she had any men in her future.

"Not really," replied Lilly. "I've struck out in that field. You know the saying 'once bitten, twice shy'? Well, I have been twice bitten, so I should be four times shy."

He asked her if she was coming back to paint. She replied she would like to. She told Bernard that when she got back, she would call Betsey to see if he was still here. Lilly said as much as she hated to, she had to go and prepare for her tour.

They got up and carried their glasses and wine back inside. Lilly turned to her easel and admired her painting. Bernard assured her it was a very good painting. Lilly was beaming and said, "I'll take it to my car and come back." Lilly secured her painting in the Jaguar and returned to get her purse.

She went over to Bernard, smiling, and gave him a big

hug, which Bernard returned. Lilly said, "I am going to miss you."

Bernard said, "I am going to miss you also."

Lilly let go of Bernard, but Bernard held on to Lilly and said very seriously,"Lilly, I may never see you again, so before you go, I want you to know that even though I have tried not to and kept my distance, I have fallen deeply in love with you."

That was the best news Lilly had had in years, and she felt the same about Bernard, but then what about Arthur, the romantic letters, and the personal poems? She wanted to melt into Bernard's arms, but needed time to sort things out. Trying to buy time, she pushed him away and said, "Bernard, don't go there."

Bernard looking lovingly at Lilly and said, "Why, Lilly, why?"

Trying to think of something to delay the situation, Lilly blurted out, "You're too old."

As soon as Lilly had said it, she was horrified at what she had just said. She wished she could have bitten off her tongue. It was just like pouring water on the ground—you can never put it back into the glass.

Bernard released her immediately, because this was why he had held back all along. As in baseball, Bernard had only one pitch to make to her, and he had made it and struck out.

Lilly, alarmed at what she had just said, was horrified at seeing the hurt look on Bernard's face. Her eyes began to fill with tears. This was the kindest man she had ever known, one who had met her every beck and call and nurtured her feelings to make her feel good about herself. Her face became contorted as the tears rolled down her cheeks. She tried to reach out and touch his cheek and make it well; however, her arm seemed frozen and unable to move. She felt as though a starving child had asked for a morsel of bread, and, in return, she had slapped his face for asking. This man had done everything he could to make her happy and did not deserve what she had said to him.

Lilly did not know what to do or how to fix it. Her inner voice said, "Run, Lilly, run." Lilly quickly turned around, grabbed her purse, and ran out the door, wishing she could hide, with the bells on the door ringing behind her.

Bernard quickly followed her as far as the big room, then watched out the large window. Lilly hurried into the car but could not get the key into the ignition because she was so upset and could not see the ignition with tears flooding her eyes. She slumped over the steering wheel, crying in despair. Bernard wanted to go to her, but he felt that as he was the one who had made her cry, it would only make matters worse. Finally, Lilly was able to get the car started, and she drove off.

Bernard turned around, went back, and leaned against the door facing by the easel. Thinking about what had just transpired, he knew she would never be back after he had made a fool of himself. In a feeling of despair, in a fleeting moment, he stood flatfooted and, with a stiff kick, kicked the paint table that held all the paint supplies over onto the floor. As the table was going over, a tube of mauve paint hit the floor first, and the table came crashing down on it, splitting the tube. All the paint supplies were scattered over the floor.

Bernard poured himself a glass of wine, went outside,

and sat in one of the café chairs. Getting his thoughts together, in a feeling of despair, he now knew he had no reason to stay. After a while, he returned inside and started to pick up the table and make it right. Then he began putting the supplies back on the table, placing everything back into the French easel except the broken tube of mauve paint, which he placed on the table on top of a piece of paper towel. He cleaned the paint off the floor.

He took the painting he had finished of Lilly holding the flowers and asked Betsey if she would keep it for him. He said someday he would return and get it. He told Betsey he had intended to give it to Lilly before she left, but things did not work out. Betsey noticed that he was not in his usual frame of mind. He was always cheerful and upbeat, but something had mentally dragged him down.

Betsey had him hang it in the dining room so it would not get damaged. He told Betsey his work there was finished, and he was going on to Europe.

Betsey asked, "What about Lilly?"

Bernard said, "She won't be coming back, so there is not any reason to stay any longer." He told her to keep and sell the finished paintings and to keep the money for all the trouble he had caused her. He told Betsey to keep the food in the refrigerator and cabinets, and the large CD player.

Betsey said, "What about the rent you have already paid?"

"I want you to keep it," replied Bernard. He asked to use her telephone. After checking the bus schedule to Dover, he made a reservation to cross the channel on the hovercraft to Belgium.

A TOUCH OF MAUVE

Hovercraft "Princess Anne," English Channel

Meanwhile, Mary heard Lilly come into the house with the rattle of the keys in the door. Lilly dropped her purse on the floor in the foyer and leaned her painting against the wall. She then leaned against the wall, exhausted, and, with the side of her head against the wall, cried with a handkerchief to her face.

Mary noticed Lilly did not come on in as she normally did. She looked up to see Lilly leaning against the wall, crying. Mary jumped up and hurried over to Lilly. Mary asked Lilly if she had had a wreck, and Lilly just shook her head no, not able to speak. Mary asked, "Did Bernard hurt you?" Lilly again shook her head no, not able to speak. Mary then asked what was wrong. Lilly again just shook her head no, because she knew she would burst out crying and she was trying to stifle that.

Mary guided Lilly over to the couch and gave her some facial tissue. It was some time before Lilly could talk. She began by telling Mary what a wonderful day it had been and that it was the best day yet. Lilly said that she had painted a beautiful painting and that they had laughed and talked, having a really fun time. "When it came time to leave, I put my painting into the car and came back to get my purse. I went over and gave Bernard a hug, and he hugged me, but he did not let go. He said 'Lilly, I may never see you again and want you to know I have fallen deeply in love with you.' Well, I was in love with him too, but I thought, what about Arthur?"

Mary, hearing that, just rolled her eyes, because she had tried to get Lilly to forget about Arthur and his letters.

Lilly said, "I was trying to buy time in case Arthur showed up. So I put my hand on his chest, pushing him away, and I told him not to go there. Then he said, 'Why, Lilly, why,' and I couldn't think of an excuse. I don't know where it came from, but I just blurted out ..."

Before Lilly could finish her sentence, Mary said, "You are too old," finishing her sentence for her.

Lilly began crying again, shaking her head yes. She said, "I don't know where it came from."

"I know," replied Mary, "you said it around here forty or fifty times."

"I know, but I didn't mean it," said Lilly, still crying. "When I saw the hurt in his face, it nearly killed me. He had never said an unkind word to me and always doted over me. Driving back, I had to stop twice because I was crying so much I couldn't see to drive. You should have seen the look on his face, I felt horrible. He did not deserve that. He spent all his time caring for me and making me happy. No man has done as much for me. I wanted to take what I said back, but I didn't know how."

"Lilly, we have to go back right now and let him know how you feel about him," said Mary.

"Oh, no! I cannot face him right now. I will go when I get back from the tour," Lilly replied.

Mary said, "Lilly, he may not be there."

Lilly replied, "He said he would stay as long as I want to paint."

Mary said, "Lilly, I think that this changes everything, but you do what you think is right for you."

After making reservations to cross the channel, Bernard went back to the garage to write Lilly a letter. He retrieved the last piece of writing paper and envelope and sat down to write. He moved the tube of mauve out of his way, not realizing that some of the mauve paint got on his hand. When he picked up the writing paper, some mauve paint got on the bottom of the page. Not having another sheet, he decided to use it anyway. He started off, "Dear Lilly, It is with great sadness that ..." and ended with "... hold you in my heart. Art."

Not thinking properly, since he had signed his other letters "Art," that was how he signed this one. He put on a stamp and, with a heavy heart, walked down the street and mailed the letter. On his return, he packed his clothes and equipment and called a taxi.

Lilly decided not to go back and see Bernard right away because she still felt too embarrassed. Instead she spent the next few days getting ready to go on tour. She spent her time making sure that the music was in order, that all her gowns were packed properly, and that Mary had the plane tickets and hotel reservations in order.

This morning she was taking it easy and waiting for Mary to bring the morning mail. It had been three days since Lilly had said her tearful goodbye to Bernard. She was lying on the bed leaning back on six pillows trying to read a magazine and trying to get over the hurt of breaking with Bernard. She was only dressed in her bra and panties, covered by a silk embroidered gown to prevent wrinkling the dress she was going to wear that day. The itinerary for the day was to go to the studio and make sure the music was in order. The tour would include France, Spain, and Italy, then back to London at the London Palladium.

Mary came in, shut the front door, and walked down the hallway toward Lilly's bedroom, humming along the way. Walking into the bedroom, she teased Lilly, "You have another love letter from Arthur."

With that, Lilly sat straight up on the side of the bed with her feet and legs handing off the side of the bed. Lilly was looking forward to reading the letter, as there was usually a poem in the letter with warm personal comments. Hoping this letter was at least as good as the other nine that she had received, she reached for the letter opener and sliced open the parchment envelope. Unfolding the letter, she began to read, with a happy smile on her face.

> *Dear Lilly,*
> *It is with great sadness that I must leave this place. I did not mean to make you cry today. I wanted to go to you when you were in the car crying, but I thought I would make matters worse since I was the one who made you cry. Our lives are like two different planets in different orbits, never to be together. I tried to keep my distance from you because of my age, but I could not help falling in love with you. You are such a wonderful person. Please forgive my transgression. I will always hold you in my heart.*
> *Art*

The smile began to turn into a frown, and her eyes began filling with tears. Puzzled at first, she reread the letter, thinking that was not Arthur, that was Bernard. Then she saw a touch of mauve paint at the bottom of the page and began to cry loudly and uncontrollably. "Oh God, No! No! No!"

She slid off the bed onto her knees and forearms, hoping the floor would swallow her up. Mary came running in, asking what was wrong. Lilly, crying, said, "It is him, it is him."

"Who?" said Mary.

"It is Bernard," Lilly answered, still crying.

Mary took the letter from her and began to read. When she finished reading, Mary said, "I don't see the connection. It's signed 'Art.' I thought you said his name was Arthur."

Lilly, still crying, said, "Art is what he does, not who he is. Look at the bottom of the page at the mauve paint."

Mary looked at the page and saw a touch of mauve paint she had not noticed before. Then she remembered what the clairvoyant had said: "The mystery will be solved with the color mauve." In plain view was a touch of mauve paint at the bottom of the page.

Lilly remembered that the details were between her and Bernard, not Arthur. She realized it would be Bernard, not Arthur, who was the one connected to the color mauve and the one who had written the letters and poems. She had rebuffed Bernard to wait for Arthur and just now found out they were the same person.

Lilly told Mary to get the car because she had to go to him. Mary told Lilly to wash her face and said she would bring the car around. Lilly washed off the mascara that had run all over her face, then put on a dress. She was ready to go by the time Mary brought the car around.

Mary drove, as Lilly was in no condition to drive, and they drove toward the little green garage. Lilly was silent most of the way, but as they crossed over a bridge, Lilly said, "Stop here, and I will drown myself in the river."

Mary said, "You are not serious. Do not be so hard on

yourself. You did not have any way of knowing he was the same person."

Arriving at the little green garage, they noticed some of the paintings were still in the window; perhaps they were not too late. They opened the door and entered to the sound of the two little bronze bells. Walking through the front toward the back, Lilly called out, "Bernard!" With no answer, they walked to the back where he painted. All the paint supplies were gone, which was a letdown for Lilly. Looking around, Lilly saw a crushed tube of mauve paint on the table. Tears began to flood her eyes as she bent down and cupped the tube of mauve paint lovingly in her hand. This had been the key to finding out who Arthur was. This was all that was left of the man she loved.

Mary pulled some tissue from an almost empty box on the table and said, "Here, put this around the tube of paint, or you will have it all over you." Mary gave Lilly more tissues to wipe the tears from her face. Mary said, "I wonder if the lady at the house knows where he has gone?"

Lilly said, "I don't know, but it won't hurt to try." They both walked down the path to the house, passing the café table and chairs where Lilly and Bernard had spent so much time eating, talking, and relaxing. Lilly, being reminded of the happy times they had spent together, only now realized how precious they were. She remembered his joking and teasing all the time. It was such a beautiful place, with all the flowers and with birds always singing.

Arriving at the house, they rang the old-fashioned bell with the twist knob. Finally, Betsey came to the door and said, "May I help you?"

Mary said, "We were wondering if you know the whereabouts of Bernard."

Betsey said, "He has gone on to Europe somewhere; he didn't say."

Mary said, "Well, his paintings are still here. Is he coming back? Lilly here wants to know."

Betsey looked around the corner of the door, saw Lilly, and said, "Oh, you are the singer that he was teaching to paint."

Lilly answered, "Yes. Did Bernard ever talk to you about me?"

Betsey, giving Lilly a puzzled look, said, "Oh, honey, you don't know, do you?"

Lilly replied, "Know what?"

Betsey opened the door wider and told the ladies to take a seat at the table on the porch. Betsey sat facing the two women. Collecting her thoughts together, looking out over the flower garden, she began to tell Lilly and Mary about Bernard. Betsey went on to tell how Bernard happened to arrive there. "He saw my flower garden through the hedge fence, and he wanted to take photographs of the flowers. Then he decided to rent the old garage and stay here a while. I told him it might not be good enough for him, but he said that it was all he needed. He found that he had left his CDs at home, so he went to the record store to buy more, and that is the first time he heard you sing. He bought a few of your records, and later he bought every album you have ever recorded."

Lilly looked at Mary, puzzled because they had only seen one CD of hers at his place.

Betsey continued, "At first, he let me hear you sing with his earphones. Then he bought a player with speakers so both of us could hear at the same time. He thought you had the most beautiful voice he ever heard. Every night, weather permitting, he would sit outside drinking his coffee and listening to your singing until dark. Sometimes he would bring the player down, and we could look out over the flower garden and listen to your music. Any time I needed any help around here, he would drop what he was doing and come help me. Even though he paid rent, he would take me down to the pub and buy my supper and he would not let me pay.

"He was like the son I never had. I wish he was still here. The day you came here, he was like a kid with a new toy. You were all he ever talked about. I knew he was getting sweet on you, and I talked to him about it. I told him he should let you know how he feels about you. He would always say he was too old."

This cut like a knife into Lilly, because those were the last words she had spoken to him.

Betsey went on, "I told him you might not feel that way about it. He said it was not fair to you to take away ten years of your life because of him when you could get a younger man."

Lilly thought to herself, yes, that's Bernard, always thinking of others first.

Betsey said, "He was all the time helping me around here. He was strong as an ox. I think that came from being raised on a farm. He gave me the finished paintings and told me to sell them and keep the money. I told him I would give him back some unused rent money, but he would not hear of it and told me to keep it.

"I think he was well off, because he had sold his businesses. Money never seemed to be an issue with him. I sure hated to see him go." Betsey sat silent for a moment, looking out over the garden and reflecting on the past. Finally, she said, "I hope I am doing the right thing." Getting up from her chair, she said, "I want to show you something in the house."

They got up and followed Betsey into the house, through the kitchen, and into the dining room, where she turned on the light and pointed to the wall. There on the wall was the portrait of Lilly in the café chair, holding a bouquet of flowers in her arms. Lilly remembered that day very well. Tears began to run down her face as she realized how much he loved her. She held her handkerchief to her face to stifle her voice and catch her tears.

Betsey said, "Every day after you left from painting, he would work on this painting. He kept it hidden and covered up so you would not see it until he finished it. He was going to give it to you before you left on your tour. Before he left for Europe, he brought it over here and asked me to hang it on the wall until he came back. He said if he doesn't come back, I should keep it. But he might want you to still have it."

Lilly said, "No, that wouldn't be right," knowing how she had rebuffed him. Lilly wanted to go somewhere and crawl into a hole. She said, "I'll wait outside." Lilly left Mary and Betsey talking as she went out, afraid she would break down in front of them. Lilly walked down the garden path to the café table and chairs. She ran her hand lovingly over the chair where Bernard always sat, remembering him and how they had laughed and talked together. Some of the best days of her life had happened here. Then, sitting down in her own chair, she leaned back and thought about how strangely everything turned out. She was in love with two men, and they turned out to be the same person. Bernard always said this place was really a paradise, only it was not the same without Bernard. There was an emptiness that was not there before. Now she realized what an important part of her life he hand become, mending and guiding her through life.

Mary came walking down the sidewalk and quietly whispered, "Lilly, it's time to go." Lilly said, "Wait a little longer," wanting to relive as many memories as she possibly could and dreading having to leave this place. Mary sat in the other seat.

Lilly was finding it hard to leave this place that Bernard loved so much. When he was here, the place was filled with joy and laughter. Now the place seemed empty without him. She alone had unknowingly caused this situation to take place. After sitting a while, reminiscing and finding it hard to leave, Lilly finally got up and proceeded to go into the garage. Remembering the sandwiches she had made for him to eat the next day, she opened the refrigerator and saw that the sandwiches were still there. She did not blame him for not taking them, knowing how hurt he was. She closed the door and went out to the car.

On the way back, Lilly was silent, and Mary asked her what she was thinking.

Lilly said, "I had a rough time when I had my two divorces, but this has almost killed me. I feel like a big part of my life is gone. The clairvoyant said that I would only have one chance, and that had come and gone."

Mary replied, "She said you would have only one chance. She didn't say that about me. Besides, Betsey gave me the address and phone number of his daughter in Tennessee."

Lilly felt a glimmer of hope that they would be able to locate Bernard. Driving back to their condominium in London, Mary said she would make the call, since it was about seven a.m. Nashville time. Mary managed to reach his daughter. She told her they had been taking art lessons from Bernard and that he left without telling them, and they were trying to get in touch with him.

Bernard's daughter said she had talked to him, but she did not know where he was going. He hade said he was going somewhere in Europe and would contact her later to let her know where he was. She told Mary to leave her phone number and, she promised she would call when she heard from him.

Mary thanked her for her help. Turning to Lilly, she relayed what Bernard's daughter had said. Lilly, being let down again, said, "This is one hell of a time to go on tour."

Mary and Lilly made their final preparations and headed out to Spain for their first leg of the tour.

Chapter 5

Lilly and Mary departed London in a 747 headed for Madrid, Spain. They were riding in first class. Mary knew Lilly was at a low ebb due to the mix-up with Bernard. She kept watching Lilly, and occasionally she would see Lilly use a handkerchief and blot a tear. Lilly was looking out the window so as not to be conspicuous.

Finally, Mary asked Lilly if she was going to be all right. Lilly smiled and said yes, she was fine. Lilly said, "I just wish I had known that Art was Bernard, and then age would not have mattered. I was thinking back that the letters stopped completely when I started painting. I do not blame Bernard. He was so deeply in love with me, but because of the age difference, he would not let himself go, and when he did, I was not ready for him. That was Bernard—he was putting me first, always. What hurt me most was when I told him he was too old. I loved him, and when I saw the hurt on his face, I almost died. Oh, he was so good to me. I hope somehow, someway, someday, I can find him."

Mary said, "I will not leave a stone unturned until I find him for you. Lay your seat back and get some rest. You will need it for the concert."

Lilly spent a good part of two days rehearsing with the orchestra in Madrid, followed by two days of concerts. The performances went well enough, but her mind was on Bernard, and she did not put as much into her performances as she normally did. The newspapers picked up on the fact that her performances were not as good as usual. At the end of each performance, she dedicated the last song to "someone special whom I dearly love." Her reviews were much the same in France and Germany, and then it was back to London.

Lilly had a three-week break before her concert at the London Palladium. Mary called Betsey to see if she had heard from Bernard, but Betsey had not. She urged Mary to call his daughter in Tennessee again, since she had already given her the telephone number. Mary called his daughter and asked if she had heard from Bernard. She replied that he had spent some time in Holland and was going on to Italy, but she did not know where. She said she would call when she found out where he was.

A few days after they had been back from Europe, Mary came into the condominium with the mail. She was upbeat, humming a song as she walked down the hall to Lilly's room and gave Lilly her mail.

Lilly asked, "What are you so happy about?"

"Oh, I don't know," said Mary. Then she asked Lilly, "Do you remember Joan Richards, the first violinist in the orchestra?"

Lilly said, "Yes."

"Well, I met her while picking up the mail. She and her husband had just gotten back from a little town called Stresa in Italy. They had been on vacation there and stayed at the Grand Hotel Bristol. She described what a beautiful place it was, right on Lake Maggiore."

Lilly was looking at Mary to see what she was getting at. She said, "So?"

"Well, she said she bought a beautiful floral painting from a yank there. I just thought you might be interested."

Lilly, wondering if this was the break she needed, said, "Call her on the phone and see who signed the painting."

Mary made several calls to Joan and finally got an answer. She told Joan Lilly wanted to know who signed the painting. Joan retrieved the painting and said, "A Bernard Anderson."

Mary said, "Thank you very much." After she hung up the phone, she told Lilly that Bernard Anderson had signed the painting.

Lilly was overjoyed, thinking there was hope. She told Mary to call their travel agent and get the next flight out and to book a suite at the hotel and get a rental car. Mary called their travel agent and told her they needed reservations for Stresa, Italy, and the Grand Hotel Bristol. She assured Mary that she would take care of it and call her back.

Lilly and Mary were busy packing their suitcases for their trip for several days' stay. About an hour later, the travel agent called and told Mary their airline tickets would be waiting at the desk the next morning. She said that the nearest airport was at Malpensa, and they would then have to drive to Stresa. She said a rental car would be waiting for them. The hotel reservations were complete with a suite on the top floor with a balcony overlooking Lake Maggiore. Mary thanked her for the quick service.

The travel agent told Mary that she wished she was going with them. She said she had been there on a promotional tour for the travel industry and it was one of the most beautiful places she had ever been to. She went on telling her that in the old days it was one of the places rich British people went to bask in the sun. In those days, London was fogged over for about a hundred years due to industrial pollution and all the houses burning coal for heat. Once corrected, London got sunshine again.

Mary thanked her and relayed the information to Lilly. They would fly out the next morning. They would have to change planes in Paris because of the short notice; however, they only had an hour's layover.

The next morning after another night of fitful sleep, Lilly and Mary ate a quick breakfast of hot tea and rolls. Mary called a taxi, and in thirty minutes, they were on their way to the airport.

After a one-hour wait, they were escorted to first class and seated. After what seemed like forever to Lilly, the doors were finally closed, and the plane taxied to the runway. Then they were airborne and glad to be off to Stresa, Italy.

On the next flight to Italy, Lilly and Mary made small talk, wondering what the weather would be like. Lilly had bought a magazine but was unable to concentrate. She kept flipping through the pages. Mainly, she just looked at the pictures. She would close it, then tap it with her fingernails, then open it again, trying to read.

One time, her tapping on the magazine was getting on Mary's nerves, and Mary reached over and politely held Lilly's hand to stop her. Lilly looked at her, then started laughing, not realizing what she had been doing. Mary told Lilly to lay her seat back, close her eyes, and relax.

It was not long before Lilly was asleep due to her tossing and turning all night, wondering about the trip. It was going to be a gamble anyway, because Bernard might not be there.

Directly the seat belt lights came on and the pilot announced they should fasten their seat belts. Lilly woke up from her sleep, looking around at Mary, and asked if they were there.

"Yes," said Mary.

Lilly started to get uptight and anxious, wondering how everything would turn out. What if Bernard was not receptive to her? What if he was not even there? The plane taxied to the gate, and everyone disembarked. They breezed through customs, then got a porter to take their luggage to the car rental and wait for them. They reported to the desk and signed for the car. A driver brought the Mercedes sedan around, and the porter put the luggage into the car. Mary tipped the porter, asking the way out of the airport and toward Stresa.

Mary, of course, was driving to allow Lilly to rest. Mary was also used to driving on the right side of the road, while Lilly had only ever driven on the left as in England.

Lilly was admiring the scenery on the way to Stresa, commenting on how beautiful the country was. The closer they got to Stresa, the more beautiful it became. She thought back to what Bernard had said:that you can make a paradise out of a lot of places. But to Lilly this place was truly a paradise, with the blue waters of Lake Maggiore, the Alps in the distance, and palm trees along the shore of the lake. Mary remarked that the travel agent said that she was envious of their going there because it was so beautiful.

They made their way through the small town of Stresa. Lilly was enjoying the view of lake as they neared the hotel. Then suddenly Lilly's heart almost stopped. Excitedly, she said, "There he is!"

Mary looked over and said, "I think you are right." She slowed the car down so Lilly could see him.

There was the love of Lilly's life, the poet and artist all rolled into one, sitting on a bench painting with his French easel. Mary drove on to the hotel and parked at the front entrance. They both got out, and Mary told the porter to take the luggage to their room and park their car, giving him the reservation number and papers.

Lilly, filled with anguish and excitement, not knowing which way things would turn out, had not taken her eyes off Bernard from the time she saw him. Lilly wanted to go to him, so they proceeded to walk across the road to the lakeside. They were some distance from Bernard when Lilly stopped, trying to get some composure. Watching Bernard sitting behind his French easel painting Lake Maggiore and the Alps, she wondered if he would even be receptive to her. She could not blame him because of the way she had insulted him by saying he was too old.

Mary whispered encouragement to Lilly, saying, "He will be more excited to see you than you are to see him. Go!" She nudged Lilly in Bernard's direction. Lilly walked slowly, partly out of fear and partly out of remorse. The nearer she got, the slower she walked, trying to build up the courage to speak with Bernard.

As Lilly neared Bernard from behind, Bernard did not think much of it, because people often watch artists in that manner and the artist pays little attention to it. Mary was taking photos to keep for Lilly. As Lilly got within touching distance, Bernard got a whiff of the perfume that he had only ever known Lilly to wear. He thought it could not be her, as she no longer had any interest in him. Besides, he had told no one where he was. Unsure of who it might be, he stopped painting and started wiping paint off his brush.

Lilly, now flooded with tears running down her face, put her right hand on his right shoulder and her right cheek against Bernard's left cheek, saying, "I'm sorry, I'm sorry," transferring her tears to his cheek. Now there was no question who that perfume belonged to. Bernard's eyes began to fill with tears, and he got up and turned around to see the most wonderful woman in the world. He quickly hugged her tightly, not letting her go. After a few moments, he released her and lightly kissed her, looking deeply into her eyes. Then he gave her a long, passionate kiss. He held on to her as if he would never let her go. Finally, he asked her what she was doing here.

Trying to make light of the situation, she grinned and told him, "My lessons. "You ran off before I finished my lessons."

Bernard said "Lilly, Lilly, Lilly!" while grinning and hugging her as tightly as he could, as if to never let her go. Then he gave her another passionate kiss. Some people passing by stopped and looked at them hugging and kissing. Bernard pulled back to see Lilly's face and surrendered all the love he had to give onto Lilly. Then, putting his cheek to hers, he held her tight for a few minutes. Lilly had never known love like this. There was no holding back. This was no ordinary man holding her in his arms.

Bernard asked her to sit down on the bench. He put his arm around her and smiled at her through his tears. Bernard asked her "How did you find me? I told no one where I was."

A TOUCH OF MAUVE

Lilly said, "I was determined to find you wherever you were. Do you remember selling a floral painting to a lady from London at the hotel?"

Bernard replied, "Yes, why?"

"She was incredibly happy with it. She is a violinist in the orchestra I perform with. She told Mary about it, and here we are." She was laughing through her tears as she said it.

Mary had been standing in the distance, wiping away her tears. Now she came up to them and said, "It looks like you two have made up, so I am going to our room. Take all the time you want, and most of all, don't hurry, as you have a lot of catching up to do."

As Mary turned away, Lilly looked at Bernard and said, "Poor Mary, I have put her through a lot in the past few months, and you are the reason why! She was so worried about me."

When Mary got to the counter, she picked up her keys and told the counter clerk to send a bottle of champagne and hors d'oeuvres to the couple on the bench by the lake and to put the tab on her room.

Lilly and Bernard looked at the Alps and the lake as they talked, taking in the beautiful surroundings. Lilly asked, "How did you find this place? It is so beautiful."

Bernard replied that he and his wife had come here on a European tour and loved this place.

Finally, Lilly, looking seriously at Bernard, in a begging mood and with tears in her eyes, asked, "Why did you not tell me you wrote those letters and poems?"

Very seriously, Bernard replied, "I could not see you being interested in me. Why would a leading singer in

Europe be interested in a common man who paints and is too old for you?"

That stung Lilly, knowing that was what she had told him even though she did not mean it. Lilly said, "Please don't ever use those words again." Shaking her head, she said, "No! You are certainly not common, and you are a wonderful man. You also paint beautiful paintings. As far as your being too old, I would rather have twenty or thirty years with you than a hundred with someone else. Betsey said any woman worth her salt would be proud to have you."

"She did?" asked Bernard.

"Yes, she said, 'Lucky is the woman that lands that man.'"

Bernard replied, "She is a grand lady with a heart of gold. I really loved her."

Two waiters showed up with a bottle of champagne and hors d'oeuvres and a small folding table. "What's this?" asked Bernard.

"Oh, that's some of Mary's doings. She wants us to celebrate. Ever since we were children, she has watched over me like a mother hen."

Bernard said, "I couldn't tell you about the letters because I had painted myself into a trap. I never expected to ever meet you. I just wanted you to know how I felt from my heart. I wanted you to know what a great singer you are and how beautiful you are. I think I fell in love with you when I saw your picture on the CD cover and even more when I met you and found out what a great personality you have. A good personality trumps beauty any day. That day you came into the little green garage where I was painting and I saw you, I almost died. I thought you had found out that I was the one writing those letters and that you had come to put a stop to it."

Lilly laughed and said, "We thought it was because you recognized me and didn't know what to say, because you didn't say a thing for a couple of minutes."

Bernard said, "I couldn't say anything. My mind went blank. I was surprised you were interested in a painting. Then, when you wanted me to teach you to paint, I was elated. I just could not believe my luck. I could not help falling in love with you, but our age difference kept me from making any advances toward you. I had no right to try to encroach upon you."

"Shush," said Lilly. "That is behind us now."

Bernard said, "That last day you were there and getting ready to go on tour, I could not stand it any longer. I decided to take my chances, because I might not ever see you again. Then when I tried to advance on you and you told me I was too old, it put me in my place. You ran out of the building and sat in the car crying. I wanted to go to you and comfort you, but I was the one who had made you cry. I felt if I went to you, I would only make matters worse. I decided it was best to leave, because there were no fences to mend. After making a fool of myself, I could not face you anymore."

"No, that was not it at all," said Lilly. "I was in love with you all along, but those letters came to me at one of the lowest points of my life. I felt, here is someone who truly loves me and understands me for who I am. When you started to kiss me, I knew I would fall deeply in love with you, and I thought I would never get a chance to meet the one who wrote those letters. I was in love with two people at the same time, and I needed time to sort things out. The reason I was crying was that I blurted out that you were too old, as that was the first thing that came to my lips and the farthest from my mind. As soon as I said it, I wished I could have bit off my tongue because I did not mean it. Oh! I cried and cried over that."

Looking up at Bernard, she started stroking his face softly with her hand, "I saw the look on your face, and it just about killed me. I knew I had hurt you, which I would not have done for anything in the world. I was crying in the car because I did not know how to fix things. I thought after the tour, when we started lessons again, I would make it up to you. How, I didn't know.

"When I got your last letter, I went to see you, and you were gone." Lilly hesitated for a minute and started to cry again. She said, "I saw that portrait you painted of me. It made me realize how much you cared about me. Did you make up those poems you sent to me?"

"Yes, Lilly, because I loved you so much."

Lilly, softly and reflectively turning to look at Bernard, said, "I have never known a man like you. As they looked at each other, she continued, "I would take six months with you over a lifetime with any other man."

Bernard replied, "We will have a lifetime from now on," and he kissed her."I painted the portrait of you because you are such a wonderful person. I wanted to capture that moment because you looked so beautiful. The flowers just added the finishing touch."

Lilly said, "When Betsey showed me the portrait it broke my heart, because those days of painting were the happiest days of my life. You showed me how to slow down and enjoy the simple things in life, such as flowers, the birds singing in the trees, and a koi pond. You showed me that I did not have to go chasing rainbows. I have never felt as comfortable with any man as I have with you. I never want it to end, and today is a new beginning."

They hugged and kissed again, and Bernard assured her he would be with her until the day he died.

Lilly said, "I need to go to my room and clean my face and fix my hair."

"Oh, you look beautiful," said Bernard. Lilly smiled, knowing how complimentary he was.

Lilly volunteered to help Bernard gather up all his gear that held painting supplies. She picked up his backpack with the wrong strap, dumping everything, and all of her CDs fell out. There was every album she had recorded. Lilly looked at Bernard and said, "You were hiding them from me."

Bernard, looking sheepish, said, "Yes, I played them all the time. I didn't want you to know how deeply I loved you, and I didn't want to persuade you; I wanted it to come from your heart."

Lilly said, "You played them for you and Betsey all the time. I wondered why I never saw them, and here they are."

They finished gathering everything up and went to the hotel. Lilly picked up her keys at the desk, and they stopped by Bernard's room of lesser value and left the art supplies in there. They continued up to Lilly's suite. Having picked up her keys, she was able to let herself and Bernard in. She called for Mary. Mary answered that she was on the balcony. They found her lying back sipping on a glass of wine, enjoying the view of Lake Maggiore.

Walking past Mary, they walked toward the edge of the balcony. The view took Lilly's breath away. They walked to the very edge and leaned against the rails, putting their arms around each other. Lilly told Bernard, "Now this is a real paradise." After looking at all the beautiful sights from the balcony, Lilly said, "I never want to leave." She then turned to Bernard like a child asking permission and said, "Can we come here to live?"

Bernard looked at her lovingly and said, "Only if you will marry me."

With that, Lilly smiled and gave Bernard a loving pinch on his stomach and said, "You know I will."

Bernard asked, "What about your career? You do your tours, and you record in London."

Lilly said, "I have one more concert, and I have enough money for two or three lifetimes. Then it will be just you and me. I will do some recordings here, and that is it. If my biological clock has not run out, I want to start a family." Lilly was silent for a moment, then said, "Bernard, Let's get married here."

Bernard replied, "I think that would be a wonderful idea."

Lilly replied, "It's such a beautiful place, and this all seems like a dream. I never want it to end." Then she looked up at Bernard with tears forming in her eyes and said how close she came to not being able to find him again.

"Now, now," said Bernard. "That's all over with. We are together again, and I know you love me. I will never leave you." He took Lilly in his arms and kissed her. Lilly looked up at him and smiled, feeling confident that what he said was true. She lay her head on his chest while enjoying the view of the lake. They held on to each other.

As they talked about their lives both past and future, taking in the beautiful view, Lilly asked Bernard, "Who lives on the two islands to the left, near the shore?"

Bernard replied, "The near one with the castle is called Isola Bella, or beautiful island."

"Oh, how romantic," said Lilly.

Isola Bella

Bernard continued, "It belongs to the Borromeo family, who still live there. For a fee, they will let you view some of the grounds. Would you and Mary like to go there?"

"Oh, yes," said Lilly, tearing up again. "This is like a dream. I can hardly believe that this is so real."

"We will go there tomorrow," said Bernard. "That would be a good day trip."

Lilly said, "Oh, I love this place so much."

Bernard said, "It's getting late. We had better go eat." They all agreed and went down to the restaurant on the main floor. They all had an enjoyable dinner of steak, lake trout, and shrimp, and the famous Italian ice cream for dessert. The waiter came and asked how the bill would be paid, all on one ticket or separate. Bernard spoke up and said all on one check and that he would take the bill. Lilly waited until the waiter walked away, then quickly put her hand on Bernard's arm and firmly told him, "From now and here forward, all the bills are to be given to Mary. She has enough credit cards to take care of everything, including your hotel room."

"But I do not want to feel as if I am mooching off you," said Bernard.

"Oh, Bernard, you don't see it, do you. You are always giving to everyone else. I know how you helped and took care of Betsey with her meals and garden. I know that is one reason I love you so. You are the first man that I have met who has not tried to mooch off me. I would appreciate it if this subject is never brought up again. I know what is in your heart, and that is why I followed you here. I make hundreds of thousands of dollars more than you, and it is the fair thing to do." When the waiter came back, Lilly took the bill and handed it to Mary, and Mary paid the bill.

Lilly wanted to go back to the suite to see the lights at night around the lake. As Bernard and Lilly walked hand in hand out on the balcony, Lilly could not believe the array of lights around Lake Maggiore. Bernard smiled at her being overjoyed by the sight.

Bernard's heart melted at the joy Lilly was having seeing the lights. He turned her to himself, kissed her, and hugged her tightly. They acted like two teenagers in love. Finally, they moved to a two-seat divan, snuggled up, and continued to hold each other while looking out over the lake at the lights. Around midnight, Bernard said, "It's time I get up and go down to my room so everyone can get some sleep."

Lilly was not used to having Bernard around. Wanting him close, she teared up and pleaded, "I almost lost you once, and you are not getting out of my sight again. There are two bedrooms here. You can take the one with the king-size bed, and Mary and I will take the one with the two queens. Now, go down and get your pajamas, and if you do not make it quick, Mary and I will be down to cause a ruckus!" They all laughed.

Bernard went down to his room and picked up his pajamas, robe, street clothes for the next day, and shaving kit and was back in no time. Mary and Lilly were already in their gowns when Bernard got back. He quickly changed out of his street clothes and into his pajamas.

Bernard and Lilly went out on the balcony one last time to look at the lights across the lake reflecting in the water. After a few hugs and kisses, they retired to their beds, dreading being apart.

Bernard lay in bed thinking of the day's events and how they came about. That morning he was all alone, and tonight he was in love with a beautiful, wonderful singer, a woman soon to be his wife. He slowly drifted off to sleep.

Lilly lay in bed finding it hard to go to sleep, wishing Bernard were by her side. She was also very thankful for how everything turned out so wonderfully. "Mary," said Lilly. "Mary, are you asleep?"

"Almost," Mary replied.

Lilly said, "Can you believe what happened today?"

Mary said, "It is hard to believe, but it all came together all right in the end."

Lilly said, "This morning I had no one, and tonight I have the most wonderful man in the world. Do you remember we were discussing what the clairvoyant said about she saw Art holding my hand? We tried to figure out who it might be. I said it couldn't be Bernard in love with me, because he only had one of my recordings."

"Yes," said Mary.

"Well, when I helped him gather up his supplies, I picked up his backpack, spilling the contents, and all of my CDs fell out. That stinker had hidden them from me so I would not know how crazy he was about me. Oh, I love him so. I am the luckiest woman in the world."

"I think you certainly are, Lilly. Now get some sleep; we have a big day tomorrow." Then they both drifted off to sleep.

Lilly awoke to find Mary already outside in her gown and robe. Lilly put on her robe and went out on the balcony with Mary, taking in the beautiful view. Bernard woke up hearing the women talking. He shaved and got into his street clothes, then went onto the balcony where Lilly was standing next to the rail. He hugged and kissed her. He was concerned if she had slept well.

She said, "Yes, after the excitement died down." Lilly said she woke up several times wondering if it was all a dream.

Bernard assured her it was not a dream, then hugged and kissed her. He asked her if they should go down and get breakfast.

"Oh, no," said Lilly. "Mary has ordered room service. Not sure what you like, she ordered ham, sausage, eggs, sweet rolls, juice, and coffee." Just then the doorbell rang. Mary went to the door and opened it. There stood the bellman with a cart loaded with food. Mary told him to leave it on the glass-top table on the balcony. Putting the food in order on the table, he left.

Bernard, though having comfortable finances, had never experienced anything as impressive as this. Lilly had Bernard sit with her and Mary on the other side so all three could enjoy the view of the Alps and Lake Maggiore. It was enjoyable watching the boats go by.

The breakfast was enjoyed by all. The food was good, and the ambiance was fantastic. It was hard for Lilly and Mary to believe such a place existed. Bernard told Lilly he would retire to his room and give them time to dress before going to the island, and he advised them not to wear high heels. To that, they all agreed. Bernard hugged and kissed Lilly, then went down to his room. After he closed the door, Lilly turned to Mary and said, "Mary, I am the happiest woman in the world. It's like being on a honeymoon." Then, on second thought, she laughed and said, "Well, almost."

Mary said, "I think you have landed a nice, wonderful man. He is only interested in you and not your money. That is a rare breed indeed."

After they dressed, they went down and collected Bernard and went on to the lobby. Bernard asked the desk manager to arrange for a boat taxi to pick them up to go to Isola Bella. The desk clerk made the call and told them it would be about fifteen minutes.

They crossed the road to the lake, then sat on the bench to wait on the water taxi. While waiting on the taxi, they admired the beauty of the place and the Alps in the background. The water taxi showed up shortly. They all boarded and were off to Isola Bella.

Mary and Lilly were enthralled at this new style of transportation. The ride was short, and they disembarked onto the island. Bernard paid for the taxi and set the time for them to be picked up and carried back to the mainland. They started walking up the hill toward the manicured grounds with an abundance of statues. The street was cobblestone, with shops lining both sides all the way up the hill.

Water Taxi

Statuary

Mary and Lilly were like two teenage girls in a candy shop. Giggling and laughing, they bought souvenirs such as scarves, bracelets, and necklaces. Lilly insisted on buying Bernard a pair of sunglasses and a European-style billed cap. She thought they made him look more distinguished.

Finally, they made their way up to the top and started touring the grounds[2], with Bernard and Lilly holding hands as they walked. Lilly spotted a white peacock strutting around the grounds. "Oh, look, Bernard, that's a good omen."

---

2 For a mini tour of Isola Bella seach "Italy+Lake Majorie+Isola Bella+Glow Travels" on YouTube

White Peacock

Bernard laughed and said, "Perhaps that means there is a wedding in our future."

Lilly looked up at him, smiled, leaned over, and rested her head on his shoulder. As they walked the grounds, Lilly held onto Bernard as if her life depended on it. She finally felt she had met a man who was her equal when it came to love, someone with the same dreams and desires as she had. She had already developed a repose with him in the many weeks they had painted together.

All three began to tire and get hungry, so they meandered their way back down toward the pier. They stopped at a small outside café and had lunch. Mary and Lilly loved the place and could not get over how quaint it was. They sat and talked for about an hour, having a leisurely lunch. Mary commented to Lilly that she had never seen her so happy, and Lilly replied that she had never been that happy. Looking at Bernard with tears welling in her eyes, knowing she had almost lost him, she leaned over, holding Bernard's hand, and kissed him.

Bernard said the taxi would return at three p.m. and they needed to make their way back to the dock. The ladies checked out another shop for souvenirs on the way back to the dock. The boat arrived on time, and they were on their way back to the hotel.

Bernard kept his arm around Lilly with her leaning on him, and they gave each other an occasional kiss. Mary, sitting behind them, kept smiling, knowing how happy Lilly was, and she took an occasional photo of them.

After they landed at the Bristol dock, while walking to the hotel, Bernard asked Lilly if Mary could go with him. He had seen a special gift he wanted to get for her. It was a special gift commemorating their getting back together here in Stresa. Lilly did not want to part with Bernard for a moment, but she thought this meant a lot to Bernard. She laughingly scolded Mary and said if she did not bring him back, she had better not come back herself. Then Lilly kissed Bernard and went into the hotel.

Mary drove Bernard to a jewelry shop he had seen while out walking around Stresa. Bernard told Mary he wanted to get Lilly something special to commemorate this occasion. Going into the jewelry shop, he looked over several jewelry cases and spotted a beautiful butterfly broach of amethysts with small rubies, emeralds and diamonds set in gold to replicate the colors of a butterfly. Pointing it out to Mary, he said he thought it was perfect. Mary said it was gorgeous and that Lilly would surely be pleased. Bernard told the clerk he would take it, but he wanted to look around. He told Mary, "Now for the real reason I came. I am going to propose to Lilly tonight."

Mary got a big smile on her face and replied, "Wow!"

He asked Mary to help him pick out a style of rings that Lilly would like. They looked over a large array of wedding and engagement rings. They finally agreed on a matching set that Lilly would like. Mary was ecstatic and could not wait to see Lilly's face when he gave them to her. Bernard told the clerk to wrap the butterfly broach and give him the rings in the box as they were.

On the way back to the hotel, he told Mary he was going to give the broach to Lilly at dinner, but he was going to propose by the lake. Mary was beside herself with excitement. Arriving back at the hotel, they went up to their suite, and Bernard went into his room in their suite, dropping off the package with the broach. He then went out on the balcony with the ladies, going over to kiss Lilly.

Lilly asked, "Did you two have a good time?"

"Oh, so-so," replied Bernard. Then he said, "It's about time to eat dinner, isn't it?"

Lilly, laughing, said, "I am so tired of walking, you may have to carry me."

"That would be my pleasure," said Bernard, grinning.

The women went to their room to freshen up, and Bernard went to his room. Putting on a jacket, he washed his hands and put the broach into his pocket and the rings in his other pocket.

Mary was excited and could barely resist telling Lilly that

Bernard was going to give her a present at dinner. Meeting at the front door, they took the elevator, with Lilly holding onto Bernard, down to the restaurant. Bernard asked the maître d' for a table that had a good view of the lake. They sat in a semicircle so all could view the lake. They ordered their drinks, and when the drinks came, they placed their food orders.

After the waiter left, Bernard reached into his jacket pocket and pulled out the gift for Lilly. Then, looking into her eyes, he said, "Lilly, if I were not to draw another breath, I want you to know how happy you have made me by coming into my life. This present is our remembrance of yesterday, the first day of our lives together."

Lilly's eyes welled with tears as she tried not to cry anymore because he was so thoughtful, and because she thought she had lost him forever. Bernard handed her the present, and her hands began to shake because of her emotion. She was having a hard time untying the ribbon because she was so nervous. Mary said, "Here," taking the ribbon off. Then Lilly unwrapped the present. When she opened it, she said it was the most beautiful thing she had ever seen. It was the beautiful butterfly broach that took her breath away. The light from the jewels was reflecting in her face.

Mary was overjoyed just watching Lilly's face. Lilly reached over, held onto Bernard's hand, squeezed it, and kissed him. She had to wipe the tears away from her face. Still looking at the broach, Lilly said, "I will keep this the rest of my life. You cannot know how much this means to me. I will cherish it forever." Lilly kept looking at Bernard, knowing no one had ever cared for her as much as Bernard did, and knowing she had almost lost him. She told Bernard, "You certainly know how to play a woman's heartstrings." Mary got up and pinned the broach on Lilly's dress.

The food came, but due to everyone's emotion, they more or less just picked at their food. Love had overcome hunger, Lilly having received the broach, and Mary and Bernard knowing he was going to propose.

Finishing their meal, Bernard suggested they all go for a walk to the lake and watch the sun go down. Mary thought that would be a great idea. Mary settled the check, and they crossed the road to the lake. They arrived at the lake and watched some boats go by, making small talk, while Mary stood behind them with her camera ready. Bernard said to Lilly, "Oh, I almost forgot, I have something to go with the broach." Reaching into his pocket, Bernard pulled out the ring box and got down on one knee as he opened the box showing Lilly what was inside. Lilly, knowing what was coming, put both of her trembling hands over her mouth and began crying, as this was unexpected. Bernard said, "I know of no other place more fitting as here on Lake Maggiore. Lilly, will you marry me?"

Lilly could not speak but was only able to shake her head yes. Mary was taking pictures in the background.

Bernard got up off his knee and placed the ring on Lilly's finger. He hugged and kissed her, tears and all. Lilly said, "Bernard, I cannot take much more of this," still crying tears of happiness. A small, intimate setting had ripped away the curtain of men's indifference toward women that Lilly had built up around her over the years.

They walked over and sat on the bench. With her head

on Bernard's shoulder and his arm around her, she continued to cry out of happiness for a few minutes. When she was able to speak, she said, "Oh, Bernard, I love you so much it hurts, but it hurts in a good way."

Bernard said, "You just don't know how much it hurt each day when you would leave me after your lessons. I had to contend with it until I could see some movement on your part because of our ages."

Bernard continued to hold her for a while. Lilly had had so many disappointments in men that this seemed unreal, and it overwhelmed her. Mary had been trying to take photos of them with tears in her eyes, and she had a hard time focusing the camera. Lilly said, "I had no idea." Then she asked Mary, "Why didn't you tell me?"

Mary said, "He made me promise I wouldn't say anything." Then she said, "It was better this way."

Bernard said, "While this proposal may seem too soon, at my age, each day counts." He looked at Lilly and said, "I think I know all about you through all the weeks we were painting together. There was never an unkind word between us. We can surely do that for the rest of our lives."

Lilly said, "You don't know how hard it was to leave you each day after we finished painting. Even though I felt drawn to you, I tried to make myself not believe it. I kept holding onto those letters, wondering who Art was, and hoping maybe someday I might meet him."

Bernard said, "I was determined not to lead you on because of my age. If anything were to happen between us, it had to be your choice. It had to be your decision if we became a couple."

As they sat and talked, they discussed where they would

be married. Lilly said, "I would like to be married in Stresa. I have never been as happy in all my life as I am here, and I would like it to continue. Mary could call around and find out about some churches."

Mary spoke up and said the hotel clerk would know of some churches. There would be dresses to make and a lot of other plans.

Lilly said, "We will take that up tomorrow. Let us turn in for the night." They returned to the hotel balcony until bedtime.

Bernard told Lilly if she did not like the rings, she could change them. She told Bernard that she loved them. "Besides," she said, "it would not have made any difference, because you picked them for me, and that is why I love them. Let us get some sleep. We have a big day tomorrow."

The next day, after a hearty breakfast on the balcony, they all went down to the hotel manager's office to gather information about a wedding planner. He named several; however, he recommended one outstanding lady. He phoned her and made an appointment for nine a.m.

Meeting with the wedding planner, they were given the name of a dressmaker and the address of a small, white stone Catholic church that performed a lot of weddings because of its quaint looks. Lilly told the wedding planner that she wanted to have the wedding dinner at the hotel, and she asked her to furnish the photographer, the cake, the dressmaker, and arrangements at the church, as well as the wedding dinner at the hotel.

They wanted to see the church to make sure it was what they wanted. Then they would go by the dressmaker to give her the particulars they wanted.

Arriving at the church, it was more than they could ask for. It was surrounded by old, large trees and a small cemetery off to one side. The building was entirely of large stone except for the windows and doors, which were of wood, and the roof, which was constructed of dark sienna tile. The stone was painted white, and the windows and large wooden doors were stained oak. The windows depicted religious figures in colored glass.

The doors being unlocked, they went inside. The church inside was even more beautiful than they had expected. The inside was white stucco, and all the woodwork was stained oak.

Hearing them talking, the rector came from the study behind the choir loft and introduced himself as the rector. Bernard reciprocated by introducing himself, Lilly, and Mary. He told the rector they were planning a wedding and named the lady in charge of planning. The rector acknowledged knowing and working with her and said would be looking forward to performing the wedding.

With their work finished there, they drove on to the dressmaker. They found the dressmaker to be a very genteel lady in her sixties. Lilly gave the dressmaker all their sizes. She showed Lilly several patterns, and Lilly settled on a waltz-length dress. The dress was to be ivory with full sleeves and accented with mauve. Mary's dress would match hers, but with opposing shades of color.

Lilly told Mary she picked mauve in remembrance of how she and Bernard got together.

"Oh, I think it will be beautiful," replied Mary.

With the wedding plans out of the way, Lilly told Mary

to go back to London and have the concert manager get a box seat by the stage for Bernard and herself. She told Mary to take the rental car back and arrange for a plane ticket for Bernard to be left at the flight ticket counter. She and Bernard would take a taxi to the airport and fly back to London the next day.

After Mary left for London, Lilly and Bernard crossed the street and sat on the park bench across from the hotel. Bernard put his arm around her shoulders with an occasional kiss to bond their love.

Bernard asked Lilly if she was sure she wanted to give up her concerts.

She replied, "Different things are important at different times of a person's life. When I was seventeen, singing and performing were the most important things in my life. I have done that for about sixteen years; I have enough money. Now, at thirty-two years of age, you are the most important thing in my life, and you will be until I draw my last breath." With that said, he leaned over and kissed her.

Lilly said, "I want to buy a small villa here on Lake Maggiore, large enough for our living quarters, a recording studio, and a painting studio for both of us. I will do all my recording there."

Bernard replied, "This all seems like a dream, something too impossible to happen. I still think back and try to understand how this all came about. With all the near misses, it is a wonder we ever got together."

The sun went down, and they decided to go to the hotel restaurant and eat. Even being engaged, she still sat as close to Bernard as possible. They enjoyed a very leisurely meal, just two people deeply in love, enjoying each other's company.

Finishing their meal, they went up to Lilly's suite. Going onto the balcony after pouring two glasses of wine, they seated themselves on a two-seat glider to be able to snuggle up and be near each other. They sat and talked until bedtime.

Lilly finally decided it was time to go to bed because they had a flight back to London. They each went to their separate bathrooms and bathed. After dressing in their nightclothes, they kissed good night. Lilly said she would turn out the lights, and they kissed again, with Lilly saying she was going to miss him.

Bernard went to his room with the king-size bed and crawled under the covers. Lilly cut out all the lights, and the next thing Bernard knew, there was a movement in the bed and he was no longer alone. Lilly was sliding in on the other side of the bed and up close to Bernard.

Bernard raised up and grinned and said, "Why, you little sneak, you."

Lilly giggled like a young girl and said, "I'm cold." With that, Bernard took her in his arms, told her he how much he loved her, and gave her a long, passionate kiss as he hugged her tightly. He lightly kissed her again. Then, while hugging her, he kissed her on her cheek, then near her ear. Then he nibbled on her ear lobe, followed by butterfly kisses down her neck. By this time, Lilly was beginning to breathe heavily. Bernard continued down her neck. As Lilly's breathing increased, Bernard kissed down her bosom to her décolletage, then the top of her breast, and then he ...

The next morning, Lilly woke up before Bernard with

a big smile on her face. She raised on one elbow and just watched her Bernard sleeping, thinking back at what he had said in one of his many talks while painting. She had asked, "How do you know when a person truly loves you." He had replied, "Never wanting to be anywhere else but with that person all the time you possibly can." He had gone on, "When I married my wife, there was no other place I wanted to be but with her. She came first. I had no outside activities that did not include her." Looking at Bernard now, Lilly now understood and had someone who would return the love that she had always yearned for and that she gave to him. Lilly thought, what if he had gone somewhere else? This would never have happened. But it did happen, and lying next to her was living proof.

After a few minutes, Bernard woke and saw tears in her eyes. He quickly raised and asked Lilly, "Why are you crying?"

Lilly said, "I am not crying; these are tears of joy." Then she leaned over and kissed him.

Bernard reached out and pulled her into his arms and kissed her, then said, "Isn't it nice to have someone to love?" Always the jokester, he added, "I was worried there for a few minutes. I thought you were going to send me back."

Lilly started laughing and playfully started beating on Bernard with her fist, "Oh, Bernard, that's why I love you." Then she hugged and kissed him. They lay there for about fifteen minutes of bliss, holding each other.

Lilly lay there thinking of her past after her father was killed in the Korean War. She missed the real love of a man. That part of her life was missing and had not been fulfilled with the men in her past. They had only used her for their benefits and who she was.

Bliss cannot last forever, and it was time to get up. Lilly told Bernard to call room service and order breakfast while she freshened up. She said that she had a rough night and felt as though she had been in a wrestling match. She gave a coy laugh, then a scream as Bernard chased her as she disappeared into the bathroom. Bernard retreated and ordered the regular fare for breakfast.

Lilly came out of her room looking fantastic, and Bernard tried to coax her back to bed.

"Oh, no, she said, "we have a plane to catch." She laughed as room service rang the doorbell. It was the bellboy with a cart loaded with breakfast. They told the bellboy to put the food on the table on the balcony. They sat down as close as they could get and enjoyed the wonderful view while eating and feeding each other breakfast.

Bernard was not accustomed to this lifestyle of Lilly's. He remarked that they were enjoying a life that most people only dream of and read about.

Lilly said, "It is a long way from the sheep pens in the Midlands where I grew up."

"Yes," said Bernard, "and a long way from the cornfields of Tennessee."

After breakfast, they went to the edge of the balcony one last time. After hugging and kissing, Bernard was not able to convince Lilly to go back to bed "for her much-needed rest." Lilly said, "It is time to go." They both got up, and Lilly packed her luggage.

Chapter 6

Mary called from London and told Lilly that the theater manager had already sold the box seat she had asked for. Lilly replied, "Mary, I have never, ever asked for a favor from those people in all the time I have performed there. Tell him that if he wants the concert to go on, I do not give a damn where he puts those people. For all I care, he can put them in chairs on the stage. If I am to perform, you and Bernard are going to be sitting in that box." With that, she hung up the phone.

Bernard came out of his room and said he was going down to his other room to pack. He would have the hotel store his painting supplies and equipment. He was back in about thirty minutes. Lilly was packed and ready. They called the bellboy to get the luggage and take it to the front desk. They loved on each other on the way down on the elevator. Lilly checked to make sure Mary had taken care of the bill, and she had Bernard's bill included in the total with theirs.

Lilly made reservations for when they returned and had the desk clerk call a taxi for them. Shortly, a taxi arrived and whisked them off to the airport. They had no trouble passing through the airport. After they were airborne, Lilly snuggled up as close to Bernard as she could get, and he did the same. She kept holding out her left hand, admiring her engagement ring. Bernard noticed her looking at her ring and said she could change it if she wanted to. She looked at him and said she loved it and that because he picked it for her it has a very special meaning to her.

Lilly was feeling that the days of anguish and searching were over. She felt completely enshrined with Bernard's love for her. She fell asleep on his shoulder and slept most of the way back to London. Waking on occasion, she would look at Bernard, feel safe and secure, and drift back to sleep. She awakened only when the plane was landing in London.

Having no delays getting through the airport, they hailed a taxi and in no time were back at her condominium. Upon their arrival, Mary greeted them and asked how their flight was. Then she told Lilly the general manager of the concert hall had called and said she could have the whole box, as it would be reserved for her use.

Bernard asked, "What was that all about?"

Lilly looked at him and said, "It was just a little bump in the road. It was the only request I have ever made. They finally came around to seeing it my way. They decided it was better to give up a few seats than to give up a whole performance."

Bernard asked Lilly, "Can we get a seat for Betsey? I think she would enjoy it. After all, she is a big part of our getting together."

Lilly hugged Bernard and said, "Mary, this is one of the reasons why I fell in love with him. He is always thinking of others." She told him, "Yes, of course, I would love to have her." She continued, "We need to see Betsey. I want her to be part of the wedding. We will go to her tomorrow and let her know how everything turned out. She does not know we got back together."

Bernard said he should go and stay in the garage until

they went back to Stresa. "Oh, no!" said Lilly, "you are staying here with me. We have a guest room you can sleep in."

The next day, Lilly and Bernard prepared to go to the little green garage to see Betsey. Lilly offered Bernard the keys to the Jaguar, but Bernard flatly refused, saying, "Oh, no. I am used to driving on the other side of the road. If I drive, we will never get there. I am not going to wreck your car." Lilly thought that was funny.

Arriving at the little green garage, they went around the side and went through the garden gate. As they rounded the corner of the garage, there was Betsey hoeing and tending to her flowers.

Bernard called out, "Hello!"

Betsey looked up and said, "Oh, my goodness!" Dropping her hoe and walking as quickly as she could in the soft garden soil, she came to greet Bernard and Lilly.

Bernard hugged her, then Lilly hugged her. Betsey said, "Oh, I am so glad to see you two together. I was afraid it would never be. Come over to the porch and sit down. I want to hear all about it."

After they were seated, Betsey wanted to hear all the details. Lilly showed her engagement ring. "Yes," said Betsey, "I looked for it when I first saw you to see if you were engaged. It is beautiful. It could never have happened to two more deserving people. I am so happy for you both. I was so sad when Bernard left, because I knew how much he loved you. How did you catch up with him?"

Lilly said, "He tried to run away, but I chased him down in Italy. We are going to be married there, and we want you to be a part of the wedding."

Betsy said, "Oh, I could never!"

"Oh yes, you can," said Lilly. "We will pay for all your expenses, and Mary will come by and pick you up so you do not worry about the trip. Give me your shoe size and dress size, and I will have your dress made there. Also, we have a seat for you at the concert this Friday night, and someone will be here in a limousine to pick you up. Give me your dress size now, and I will have a dress sent to you for the concert."

"Oh, I don't know what to say. I have never been to a big concert before, and I have never been on a plane or out of England, either," she said, laughing.

"You don't need to worry. We will take care of everything. Mary will pick you up and fly with you to Stresa so you will not be by yourself. We will send you a date and time so that you will be ready."Betsey could not believe someone as famous as Lily would include her at her wedding. They gave Betsey their phone number so she could check in with them if she needed more information. They both hugged Betsey and bid her goodbye, and they said they would see her Friday at the concert.

On the way back, Lilly stopped at a clothier and had Bernard pick out a suit for the concert. She thought Bernard looked distinguished in a suit. The only things she had ever seen him in were his painting clothes and street clothes. After picking out Bernard's suit, Lilly started to pay for it and Betsey's dress.

Bernard said no, he would pay for his, because it was for him.

Lilly replied, "Bernard, please, do not question what I do for you. It is my pleasure to do things for you."

Bernard said, "I feel badly not paying my way."

Lilly replied, "I can never repay you for what you have done for me. This is the way I show my love for you."

She picked out a beautiful dress for Betsey to wear to the concert, an outer jacket to go with it and shoes to match. She gave them Betsey's address and asked them to deliver it.

Bernard said, "I love you for being so gracious to Betsey." Lilly said, "I had a good teacher," and she kissed him.

Friday, the day of the concert, Mary called Betsey and told her when the limousine would pick her up. Mary said she would meet Betsey at the door of the concert hall and show her to her seat.

Lilly, Bernard, and Mary were driven down in another limousine so they would not have to worry about parking. They all went to the stage door. Mary and Bernard were escorted to their box seats. Lilly went into her dressing room for her make-up and her gown for the performance.

Finding his way to their box, Bernard took a seat, and Mary went on to the front door to meet Betsey. Soon she was back with Betsey. As Betsey entered the box looking down and around the concert hall, she said, "Well, I never!"

Bernard turned around, looked at Betsey, and, laughing, said, "I have never either!"

Bernard bragged on how good Betsey looked. He teased her, saying, "If I had known you looked that good, I would have married you."

Betsey said, "I have never had a dress this nice, nor a corsage like this one that Mary brought me."

"You look beautiful," said Bernard, which brought a big smile to Betsey's face.

Betsey took a seat and was beside herself watching all the well-dressed people coming in and being seated. Bernard gave Betsey a program of the evening performance and the line-up of the songs.

Bernard was excited because he had never seen Lilly perform. Soon the lights were dimmed, and everyone got quiet. The orchestra started playing the prelude. The curtains slowly opened, showing the orchestra and back-up singers. Then, down the stairs came Lilly in a beautiful gown and all her glory.

Betsey whispered, "Oh, look how beautiful she is." Bernard could not believe how beautiful she looked in that beautiful gown and a beautiful corsage with a mauve ribbon.

Lilly was looking at their box to get their approval. Bernard could not believe he was the recipient of such a beautiful and talented woman.

Lilly gave an outstanding performance for the first half of the concert. She kept looking up at the box where Bernard sat. Some of the people became aware of it and wondered whom she kept looking toward. During the intermission, Lilly came up to the box and briefly saw Bernard to get his approval and to brag on Betsey on how beautiful she looked. She told Betsey, "My, you are the belle of the ball." Betsey thanked her. Lilly quickly returned to the backstage for the final act of the concert.

Betsey told Bernard, "She is the loveliest woman I ever met. It took a man like you to bring out the best in her."

Lilly had arranged with Mary to have her bring Bernard and Betsey down to the side backstage when she did her encores. Mary, watching the program, saw the last number coming up and told Bernard and Betsey they were to meet Lilly backstage by the end of the last number. They made their way to the stairs just off the curtain where Lilly took her bows and encores.

At the end of the last number, Lilly started taking her bows as the curtain opened and closed after each bow. As she took each bow, she would walk near Bernard, then back out and take a bow. Knowing Bernard would never voluntarily go on stage, on the next to the last bow she came over and gave Bernard a quick kiss, then, holding his hand very tightly, pulled him out on the stage just as the curtain began to open for the last time.

Bernard was horrified, as this was unexpected. The crowd grew quiet, trying to understand what was going on. Lilly said, "Ladies and gentlemen, I want to introduce to you the most important person in my life: my fiancé, Bernard Anderson. We are to be married this month."

The crowd went wild and yelled and clapped for them. Lilly turned to Bernard and gave him a great big kiss as the curtain closed. Mary and Betsey were standing to the side with tears running down their faces. Although Bernard did not approve of what Lilly had done and would not have volunteered to go onstage, he knew it was important to Lilly. He loved her so much, it did not matter.

Lilly took them back to her dressing room, which by this time was filled with flowers, and asked that the flowers be taken to the nursing home where Betsey took flowers, and in Betsey's name. Then they all went out to their waiting limousine and were whisked off to one of London's posh restaurants for an evening meal and celebration.

Mary had made all the arrangements for their dinner party ahead of time. Being dropped off at the front door of a restaurant from a limousine was sure impressing Betsey, and it was all new to Bernard also.

They were escorted over to their private table and seated. Some of the people around them recognized Lilly. Being the jokester she was, Betsey leaned over to Bernard and said, "This is the first time I have ever been anybody." Bernard burst out laughing. Lilly, smiling, asked Bernard what Betsey had said. When Bernard told her, she burst out laughing. Lilly said, "Betsey, you are a very important somebody to us."

Bernard and Betsey were both amazed at the service and the variety of foods being served. The party went on until two a.m. They finally decided to call it a night, and they piled into the limousine and headed to their condominium. Arriving at their condominium, they told the limousine driver to take Betsey to her home. They told Betsey they would be in touch about the wedding arrangements. As soon as they got inside, they all sat down and kicked off their shoes. Lilly was both glad and sad at the same time: sad that she would not be performing again, and glad that she could spend all her time with Bernard.

Bernard and Lilly were sitting on the couch, and Bernard pulled Lilly over to him and put his arm around her. He said, "That was a wonderful performance tonight, and I was proud of you." He kissed her and continued, "I cannot thank you enough for what you did for Betsey. Thanks to you, you let her experience something that she could never have done on her own. She was able to travel from a mundane life into a life people only dream about. You did it for someone who can never repay you, and I admire you and I love you for it."

Lilly said, "It would never have happened except for you." They both hugged and kissed.

Bernard said, "It's time to turn in for the night, so I will go to my room."

Lilly jokingly said, "Bernard, I had the maid measure my bed, and she said there is enough room in that king-size bed for two people. From here on, I am not sleeping by myself. So get your gear and move it into my bedroom." Mary was about to fall out of her chair laughing.

Bernard, caught off guard, looked around at Mary sitting there and wondered what Mary would think, since he and Lilly were not married. Thinking about how it would be perceived by Mary, he said, "What about Mary?"

Lilly, seeing an opening in the way he said it, thought she would have some fun, as Bernard was easily embarrassed. Lilly said, "Mary's going to sleep in her bed."

Bernard turned red in the face and said, "That's not what I meant."

"I know what you meant," said Lilly. Mary was rolling in laughter, about to fall out of her chair. Embarrassed now, Bernard said, "I meant what is Mary going to think?"

Lilly said, "I don't care what she thinks. I have already told her about the day she left for London and how you enticed me into your bed and ravished me and had your way with me." Mary was still laughing, and Lilly joined in the laughter as well.

Bernard, finding he was the butt of the joke, took Lilly

into his arms and said, "What am I getting into? I can handle one of you, but when the two of you get together, I am helpless. I thought for a minute I was going to have to call Betsey to come and get me."

Lilly loved on Bernard and led him into the bedroom. They changed into their nightclothes, and Bernard crawled into the bed first. Lilly slid in on the other side and crawled over to Bernard on her stomach and elbows. Running her fingers through his hair, she said, "I once asked a wise sage how you know when you truly love someone. He told me when you want to spend every minute and hour you can with that person. Well, that's where I am and how I feel now."

Bernard smiled, remembering he was the one who had told her that.

Lilly said, "He was wise beyond his years, and I am following his advice. That is why you are here in bed with me. I want to spend every moment I can with you. At this stage of my life, I do not care what someone else thinks. It is the time we can be together that counts. As for Mary, she could see right away that I was in love with you. She tried her best to get me to marry you when I first started painting with you." She leaned over and kissed him. "Now, let us get some sleep. It has been a very tiring day for me. We need to start planning for Stresa tomorrow." She laid her head on his arm, he pulled her into his arms, and they went to sleep.

Chapter 7

It was slow moving for the three individuals at Lilly's condominium. It was getting close to 10:30 a.m., and Bernard was still sound asleep. Lilly was trying to move but was stiff and sore from the pent-up tension of putting on a concert. Bernard felt her movement in the bed and began to wake up. Remembering he had gone to bed with Lilly, he reached over and pulled Lilly to him. Lilly reached out and returned the hug with a smile on her lips.

They lay there another twenty minutes, holding on to each other. Lilly asked Bernard how well he had slept.

"Very good," he replied. "I will always sleep well when you are next to me. How did you sleep?" he asked.

"I tossed and turned because of the tension I was under. It's over now. I do not think I will miss it. There is a lot that goes into putting on a show. The tension comes from thinking you are liable to screw something up. How about a cup of hot coffee or tea?"

Bernard said, "I'll take coffee. I never could drink hot tea. That is all the Newfoundlanders made while I was stationed in Labrador. It tasted too much like the black-drought our mother gave us kids as a laxative."

Lilly laughed and said, "Let's head for the kitchen."

Mary, always the early riser, was in the kitchen nook drinking hot tea. Lilly started kidding Bernard again. She told Mary, "Well he did it again! He snuck into my bed last night."

"I know," said Mary. "He's pretty slick. You will have to watch him."

Bernard, with a smile on his face, said, "I'm going to move back to Betsey's garage to get you two to stop picking on me."

Lilly said, "I go where you go. It will be pretty tight with two people sleeping on that single bed." Mary almost spat out the tea she was drinking.

Lilly hugged and kissed Bernard, saying, "I love you."

"I know you do. That is the only reason I put up with your teasing," Bernard replied.

Lilly asked Bernard if he would like an English muffin with a poached egg on top. Bernard said, "I'll pass on that. We cook our eggs where I come from. Just toast two sides of the muffin, and I'll have jelly and coffee."

While eating breakfast, Lilly told Mary to get the travel agent to make plane and rental car reservations for Wednesday or Thursday, then to call the Grand Hotel Bristol, as they were holding the suite for them. Meanwhile, Lilly and Bernard would go to a few art museums to get ideas and look at different art.

Finishing breakfast, they went to separate bathrooms to get ready. Mary stayed behind to catch up on the books while Bernard and Lilly took in the art museum.

They met up with Mary at a restaurant for lunch. Mary said reservations had been made for Lilly and Bernard to fly out on Wednesday and that the suite would be ready. Lilly told Mary she would be buying some real estate and an automobile, and she asked her to transfer funds to a bank in Stresa. She was going to have to open a checking account with two credit cards.

Lilly and Bernard spent Sunday, Monday, and Tuesday going to museums, just taking it easy and enjoying each other's company.

During lunch on Tuesday, Bernard said to Lilly, "Let us call Betsey and tell her we will pick her up and go to the pub near her, the one where she goes. I do not want you to disguise yourself. Let the customers see Betsey with you. That would be something she would be proud of, and she would talk about it for years."

Lilly said, "I think that would be great and a fun thing to do for her."

Bernard said, "You dial her number, but I will talk to her as though I will be the only one coming."

Betsey answered the phone, and Bernard said he would be around to take her to supper at six o'clock that evening. She was happy to hear from him, and she said she would be waiting.

Lilly and Bernard spent the rest of the afternoon shopping. At five in the afternoon, they got into the powder-blue Jaguar and started for Betsey's place. They parked where Lilly always parked, and they went around the garage and through the garden gate.

Betsey was waiting in her chair on the back porch. On seeing Lilly with Bernard, she sat there with her mouth open in wonderment. She was overwhelmed to see Lilly, as she had thought only Bernard was coming. Lilly and Bernard were all smiles, seeing Betsey's surprised look.

Betsey got up and hugged them both, telling Lilly, "Honey, you are not going over there, are you?"

"I sure am," said Lilly.

"Oh, my goodness," said Betsey. "That place is not good enough for you."

Lilly said, "Betsey, any place you go is good enough for me." They all walked the short distance to the pub.

Betsey went in first with a big smile on her face, wondering what the regulars would think of her coming in with someone famous. Lilly came in next, and the regulars started whispering to each other as most of them recognized Lilly. Bernard came in right behind her.

Bernard moved them to a table in the back. Betsey was beaming ear to ear, seeing the people staring at them. They knew Betsey was somebody now because of the company she was with.

Bernard placed their order at the bar, and then they took a seat waiting for their meal. Instead of the bartender calling them to pick up their food, he brought it around the counter to them. He acknowledged Betsey by calling her "Miss Betsey." Betsey could hardly keep a straight face. He asked if there was anything else, he could do for them. Bernard, thanking him, said, "No, that will be all."

While they were eating, people kept staring at them and whispering back and forth. When they finished their meal, the bartender came over with a menu and said "Miss Lilly, would you mind signing this menu? I would like to hang it on the wall, if you don't mind."

"I don't mind at all, and I am glad to." Then she signed the menu for him.

He said, "This will mean a lot for our business," then thanked her.

Several others, seeing that, brought sundry items for

Lilly to sign. Betsey was so proud, it seemed the buttons on her dress would pop off.

Finishing their drinks, they got up and went toward the door, with every eye in the place on them. As they were walking back to Betsey's place, Bernard said, "Betsey, you are going to be a popular person in that pub from now on. You probably will not ever have to pay for another pint."

Betsey was laughing. "They sure brought our food in a hurry. I do not know how I will ever repay you for all you have done for me."

Bernard said, "Betsey, if it wasn't for you, Lilly and I would not be together."

They walked Betsey up to her door. She asked them to come in, but they declined and said they had a plane to catch in the morning. Lilly spoke up by asking Bernard if they could take her portrait with them. "Oh, yes," said Betsey. "Bernard, come in here and take it down off the wall." Bernard and Lilly went with Betsey to the dining room and took down the portrait from the wall. Lilly was in a better frame of mind than the last time she had seen it. They thanked her for keeping it for them. They said the next time they would see her would be in Italy.

They said their goodbyes and walked down the winding path that Bernard had walked so many times. They stopped at the gate before they opened it and looked around at Betsey's beautiful flower garden. Bernard put his arm around Lilly and said, "This is where it all began."

Lilly leaned over on him and said, "We had such wonderful times here."

Bernard said, "It almost killed me each time you left."

Lilly said, "It didn't do me any good, either."

They opened the gate and went to the car. Bernard placed Lilly's portrait behind Lilly's car seat to keep it from getting damaged. Before closing the car door, he reached in and hugged Lilly saying, "I love you," and he kissed her. Looking into her eyes, tears came to his. He said, "Lilly, you did a grand thing for Betsey tonight, and I love you for it. She will be talking about it for the rest of her life."

Lilly said, "Bernard, I did it for you as well as Betsey. I see how you treat the poorer people, which we both were at one time, but you still seem to be attached to it." After another round of kisses, Bernard got into the car, and they drove off to Lilly's condominium.

When they arrived, Mary was in her chair. She greeted them and wanted to know what they had been up to. Bernard had Lilly tell Mary how they had taken Betsey to eat in her local pub and how proud it made her.

Mary said, "Oh, how sweet."

After talking for a while, Lilly said, "We had better go to bed. We have a long day tomorrow. We need to finish packing." Lilly turned to Bernard and said, "Do you know which bed you are sleeping in tonight?"

Bernard replied, "I think I have that down pat."

Mary laughed in the background.

They turned in for the night, and Lilly, getting into bed with Bernard, was happy to have the love of her life right beside her.

Chapter 8

Hurrying through breakfast the next morning, Lilly and Bernard finished packing the clothes they would need until Mary sent the bulk of her clothes by freight.

Mary was staying in London running Lilly's business, and on some occasions she would be in Stresa. As a result, Lilly left enough clothes behind for use when in London, telling Mary they would see her in Stresa.

A taxi was called, and they were whisked off to the airport. Arriving at the airport, they picked up their waiting tickets, and as soon as their flight was announced, they boarded in first class. This new lifestyle was new to Bernard, as he always flew tourist seating. In no time, they were airborne to Lilly's new life with Bernard and the beautiful country around Lake Maggiore.

Now she had someone to love who was the real thing, someone she knew would give her one hundred percent of his love. She slowly drifted off to sleep.

About an hour into the flight, Lilly began to wake. Waking up a little disoriented, she looked up at Bernard, gave him a big smile, and asked if they were there yet. "Almost," he replied. "About a half hour out." She kissed him and said, "I can't wait. It will be a new beginning."

In just a little while, the bells rang and lights flash to fasten seatbelts. After landing, they exited the plane and went through customs with their luggage, then on to the car rental. Lilly had Bernard sign out for the car, because he was used to driving on the right side of the road—or, as Bernard would tease her, "the proper side of the road."

After loading their luggage into the Mercedes, they were on their way to Stresa. While driving, Lilly told Bernard that they had several things to do. They had to check on how the preparations for the wedding were going. They had to buy a villa, buy a new car, and finish setting up a bank account. She said she had already had Mary set up an account with an Italian bank with several million pounds for them to work with. They just needed to leave their signatures and pick up some cash, checks, and new credit cards.

As they came into a small Italian village, Lilly spotted a restaurant by the lake with outdoor tables. She said, "Let us stop here. It is so nice and romantic. We are on our own time, and we have the rest of our lives to enjoy." Stopping at the restaurant, they were greeted at the door by a lady who asked their seating preferences. They asked if they could sit outside and eat at the tables on the patio. The lady acknowledged by nodding her head yes. Shortly after they were seated, a waitress came with the menus, and they pointed to the items they wanted. She indicated she understood and left to get their food.

Lilly said, "Isn't this romantic? It is like being on vacation for the rest of our lives. The whole country is beautiful here in the northern part of Italy."

The waitress brought their food. While eating, they watched the boats go by. Bernard commented on the food being delicious. Lilly agreed and said the lakeside made it a perfect stop.

After finishing their food and paying their bill, they walked over to a park bench near the lake and sat down. Bernard sat with his arm around Lilly, and occasionally he would kiss her. Then he started nibbling on her ear. Shortly, she turned to him and said, "Bernard, with all our luggage, there is not enough room in that car for what you're after. I can get a motel room, and we will not get to Stresa until tomorrow." Bernard began laughing so hard he almost fell off the bench. They decided it was time to continue their trip to Stresa. They had enjoyed a perfect meal and loved the location near the water.

Finally arriving at the Grand Hotel Bristol, they had a bellhop unload the luggage and take it up to their suite. Lilly took care of the paperwork while Bernard parked the car.

Grand Hotel Bristol

On entering their suite, they went directly to the edge of the balcony to enjoy the view of Lake Maggiore. With Bernard's arm around her, Lilly turned to Bernard to express how happy she was and how much she loved him. "I am so happy to be back here. It is like a dream."

Bernard said, "Lilly, it would be impossible for you to understand the depth of love I have for you. It is hard to understand myself. It is because you are so beautiful, so talented, and such a giving person. I never want to be without you."

Lilly's eyes began to fill with tears. She looked at him and said, "Bernard, you sure know the right buttons to push in a woman's mind. I cannot go on forever crying like this, even though they are tears of joy." Wiping her eyes, she said, "We need to unpack. It's getting close to the evening meal."

Arriving at the restaurant, Bernard asked for a window seat so they could enjoy the view of the lake. Over dinner, Lilly said, "Tomorrow, we will go to the bank and take care of the paperwork. After that, we will go to the car dealership to get our own automobile, and then we will return the rental car. Tomorrow or the next day, we have to go to the dressmaker's and see how far along she is on making the dresses for the wedding."

After dinner, they went across the street and sat on the bench. They wanted to relive their meeting there two weeks ago. Lilly said, "When I saw you sitting here on this bench, my heart was in my throat because I thought I would never see you again. What if you had gone on to the rest of your trip? We would not be sitting here now. I shudder to think I might have missed finding you. Then, as I walked over here that day, I thought you might reject me because of how I insulted you."

Bernard tightened his arm around her and said, "I could never have rejected you, for I loved you so much."

Lilly said, "I was so happy when we hugged and kissed, and this place is so beautiful. It was like a fairy tale. I never want to lose that moment and that feeling. That is why I wanted to come here to live."

They went back to the suite. After sitting and talking for a while, they decided to turn in for the night.

The next morning after breakfast, they asked the desk clerk the directions to the bank branch where Mary had set up the account. Arriving at the bank, they found a bank employee who could speak English and take care of their business. They received a fair amount of Italian lira and two credit cards, one for Lilly and one for Bernard. Bernard objected, saying he should not have a credit card on her account. Lilly laughed and said, "You will have to take that up with Mary. She makes all the money decisions."

Having taken care of their banking requirements, they drove over to the car dealership. Bernard asked her, "What about your Jaguar?"

Lilly replied, "It will stay in London for Mary to use. Besides, the steering wheel is on the right-hand side of the car, making it more difficult to drive in Italy."

On arriving at the dealership, they proceeded to look around at the Mercedes and Maseratis with the help of a salesman. She told Bernard to pick out one that he liked, adding that it would be just for him. Bernard said, "Oh, no, you are not buying me a car. They are much too expensive. Besides, I can buy one on my own."

Lilly told the salesman they needed to be alone for a few minutes. "Please excuse us, and we will get back to you." The salesman said he understood and walked away. She looked at Bernard with tears forming in her eyes and said, "Do you remember the poems you wrote to me?"

"Yes," said Bernard.

"Do you remember the portrait you painted for me?"

"Yes."

"Do you remember the trip you cut short to teach me art?"

"Yes."

"Do you remember getting on your knee and proposing to me?"

"Yes," said Bernard, not understanding where she was going with the conversation.

Then she said, "Those are things that can't be bought. They are priceless. You did all of that because of your love for me, and that is why I love you. This car is something that can be bought and something I can afford. It is your wedding present, and I want you to pick one out that you will be proud of. I had two husbands whom I couldn't keep out of my bank account, and now I can't get you into it."

Bernard said, "I just don't want to take your money."

"You are not taking it. I am giving it to you. That bank account is for both of us, because I know enough about you to know you will protect it more than I would."

Bernard hugged her and told her he loved her. They told the salesman they were ready. Bernard started looking at the Mercedes, but Lilly steered him over to the Maseratis, where he reluctantly picked out a silver sedan, as it would be more useful to drive around the lake area. When they signed the paperwork, the salesman asked Lilly if she had a particular bank she wanted to finance it with. She told him that she would pay cash, and she wrote out a check for the full amount. The salesman seemed startled. Lilly looked at Bernard and said, "My fiancé has just come into a lot of money." All Bernard could do was smile, shake his head, and look away. Lilly asked the salesman if she could leave the rental car there until they came and picked it up. He said that would be fine. With that, he gave them the keys, and they went outside. Lilly said, "Please forgive me. I love to tease you, but it is because I love you."

They drove off in the direction of the dressmaker's, with Bernard feeling very much out of place. Lilly asked him how he liked his new car.

"It is wonderful, but I am speechless."

Lilly said, "Bernard, this is how I see you, and I want no less for you."

After having lunch at a small Italian café, they drove to the tailor and dressmaker's shop. The lady in the shop was glad to see them. She wanted them to try on their clothes for a perfect fit. Bernard's suit jacket needed a little tightening in the small of the back, but the shirt was perfect. Lilly had Bernard sit in the waiting room so he could not see the wedding dress until the wedding. The dress was nearly a perfect fit except for a little tightening in the waist. The lady had their shoes and stockings. Lilly's hat was perfect, except that the pearls were yet to be sewn into the netting, and the embroidery and lace had yet to be added on the sleeves and bodice. The lady told them to come back in two days for the final fitting. She said the clothes would be at the church on the day of the wedding. They thanked the lady and headed back to the hotel.

Lilly loved sitting on the balcony and looking at Lake Maggiore. While sitting on the divan, she reminisced. She told Bernard how she and Mary had laughed when they first walked into the little green garage, and he was speechless. Bernard grinned and said, "I was horrified. I had been writing to you, and you came into the studio and asked about art. I had no idea what you were talking about. My thought was, why is she here? Is she going to put a stop to those letters and tell me off? I was deeply in love with you, and to you, I was a nobody."

Lilly said, "It may have started with a laugh, but you sure worked miracles to make me fall in love with you." Then Lilly asked Bernard, "Are you looking forward to the wedding?"

"Yes, very much so. Anyone would be happy to marry you."

"The same goes for you," said Lilly. "We could go on living as we are and be happy, but marriage shows commitment. I want the world to know I am committed to your life, and your marriage to me shows you are committed to me and my life. Tomorrow, we will call the real estate lady and see if she has found some properties to check out. We need to call the wedding planner and touch base with her."

Bernard suggested they go down for the evening meal, for it had been a full day. As usual, Bernard asked for a window seat, which they gladly provided. Lilly loved looking at the lake while dining. The house lights seemed to twinkle in the distance due to the warm and cool layers of air causing a distortion in the lights.

After their dinner, Lilly said, "Let's go over and sit on our bench." Arriving at the lake, they sat on the bench, with Bernard's arm around Lilly. Lilly said, "This is a special place for me. It has the most beautiful memories. It holds a special place in my heart. I had found you, but I was not sure what to expect. Then you accepted me with open arms. That was the most joyful time of my life. Then you proposed to me here. To me, it is almost like a holy shrine."

Bernard said, "I was astonished because I never expected to ever see you again. I still held you in my heart, but I thought it was not to be. I had to get away because I could not endure being near you and unable to touch you."

After about an hour of reminiscing, they turned in for the night, leaving a wake-up call for seven a.m. The favorite time of day for Lilly was to be able to get in bed with Bernard and snuggle up in his arms. She felt so loved and secure.

The wake-up call came at seven the next morning. Bernard ordered their usual breakfast to be delivered to the balcony. After breakfast, Lilly called the wedding planner, who assured her everything was going fine. Lilly told her to hire a singer, and she said she wanted some words that Bernard had written for her called "The Wedding Promise," included in the ceremony. She said, "I will bring them to you." Next, Lilly called the real estate lady and asked if she had found any properties for her to look at. She replied that she had found four, but only three were exceptional. She added that she could show the two that were unoccupied that morning. Lilly agreed, and the real estate lady said she would pick them up at ten a.m.

Lilly did not think much of the first one, but she fell in love with the second one. It had been repainted and redecorated throughout, and all the appliances were new. It was built into the side of a rocky outcrop on Lake Maggiore. The main house was two stories at ground level, but it had two large rooms built as recreation rooms with baths that descended to the water, with one above the other. Lilly said the upper room could be her recording studio, and the lower one could be the painting studio. It had a boat slip for a boat if so desired, and there was a good size deck with patio furniture.

Lilly asked the real estate lady the price. She told her in lira, and Lilly asked what that would be in English pounds. The real estate lady gave her the total in several million pounds. Lilly asked Bernard what he thought of the place. Bernard said he loved it, especially because the art studio had north-facing light. He told her that was a tremendous amount of money. Lilly said, "It's for us, for the rest of our lives." Lilly told the lady they would take it. The real estate lady asked her which bank she wanted to finance it with. Lilly said, "We will pay cash." The lady looked startled. Then Lilly, looking at Bernard and smiling, said, "We can afford it. My fiancé is coming into a lot of money." The only thing Bernard could do was smile and turn his head. Lilly liked playing jokes on him, as he was easily embarrassed.

The real estate lady said, "Lucky for him." Bernard had to turn his back to them to keep from laughing.

Lilly asked the lady if she could recommend a house decorator, as they had no furnishings. The real estate lady said she would have one call her. Lilly asked the lady if she would leave them for a few minutes to look around. She said she would wait in the car.

After she left, Lilly turned and looked at Bernard and said, "What do you think?"

Bernard replied, "I'm in over my head."

Lilly said, "Well, you are inheriting a lot of money when you marry me, aren't you?"

Bernard took her in his arms and, smiling, said, "Lilly, Lilly, what am I going to do with you?" He kissed her and said, "I didn't realize I was marrying the Bank of England."

Lilly said, "I just love it when I can embarrass you." Then she said, "Can you be happy here?"

Bernard said, "I could be happy living in a mud shack as long as I have you."

"Wait until I tell Mary you persuaded me to spend all this money.", said Lilly.

"I'm sure you will," said Bernard, smiling because he knew how they loved to gang up on him to embarrass him.

"Do you like the house as a whole?" asked Lilly.

"Oh, it is wonderful. It is beyond anything that I could have imagined," said Bernard, "with eight bedrooms, ten baths, den, formal living and dining rooms, and a very expensive car. I hope you will not be disappointed after doing all this."

Lilly said, "Bernard, you have made me so happy—and I love you so much—that if I lost it all tomorrow, it would be worth it. You can repay me with three words."

Bernard said, "I know what they are. I love you ... with all my soul and every ounce of my body." He took her in his arms and held her.

Lilly said, "Let us get out of here. We have a lot of work to do. I would like for us to spend our honeymoon in Paris, would you?"

"Yes," he replied.

On the way back to the hotel, the real estate lady said she would call when the paperwork was ready. Lilly asked for two copies of the floor plan so she could go over it with the decorator.

In about an hour, the home decorator called and asked to meet with her. Lilly said to come to their suite at the hotel. The lady arrived with a load of books on furniture, paints, curtains, carpets, decorations, and everything else one would need to decorate a house. She had stopped by the real estate office and picked up the house plans to work with.

Lilly picked out the furnishings for the house. She wanted to put Bernard's painting of the white Rose of Sharon and monarch butterfly in the living room. The mauve Rose of Sharon with the goldfinch would go in the master bedroom, along with the yellow and orange poppies.

LARRY MORRISON VADEN

White Rose of Sharon with Butterfly

A TOUCH OF MAUVE

Mauve Rose of Sharon with Goldfinch

LARRY MORRISON VADEN

Poppies

Lilly left it up to the decorator for any needed changes in drapes or carpet as well as painting. She told the decorator she had a week to finish the house. The decorator said she was sure it could be finished by then, adding, "You sure are spending a lot of money, but it will be beautiful."

Lilly, looking at Bernard, replied, "My fiancé is doing all this to show his love for me."

"You sure are a lucky woman."

After the lady left, Lilly, grinning, went over to Bernard, sat down, and put her arm around him. She said, "I do love you."

Bernard said, "Is this what my life is going to be like?"

"Mostly," said Lilly, pinching his cheek. "It is your fault I am spending all this money. If you had not sent those letters and poems to me, this would not have happened." Then she got teary-eyed and serious and said, "You don't know how happy you have made me, just you, being in love with me. I just revel in every day I am with you. Forgive me for teasing you, but I do it because I love you. I look back over my life and realize I did not know what real love was until I lost you. I shudder to think what my life would be like if I hadn't found you."

With nothing to do but wait for the villa and wedding preparations, Lilly suggested they go back to Isola Bella and see the baroque Borromeo Palace. They had spent the last time going through the shops and the manicured grounds with the hedges and all the statues. Bernard thought that would be great.

The next morning, they had an early wake-up call and breakfast on the balcony. Lilly could not get enough of the view of Lake Maggiore.

After breakfast, they went down to the lobby and had the clerk ring for a water taxi. The taxi arrived on time, and they had an enjoyable trip to the island. This time, they went directly to the palace, deciding to join the guided tour but hanging back from the crowd so as to be left alone.

Lilly was not prepared for what she was seeing. She had seen palaces before, but this one was extraordinary. This one had ornate ceilings, gold leaf arches, and woodwork, ornate chairs, and inlaid tables. tapestries and gold leaf framed pictures were hung from floor to ceiling. Some ceilings were twenty feet high, with beautiful chandeliers. At the downstairs lake level, beautiful walls and arches were covered with different sizes and types of seashells, and the floors were inlaid with beautiful designs of river stones. In summer, this was where the occupants spent their leisure time, as it was open to the lake and a cool breeze flowed through the building.

At the end of the tour, they decided to eat lunch at an Italian restaurant near the castle. They were overjoyed by the good Italian-style food. After lunch, they went shopping at the shops and outside vendors in the commercial district. Bernard bought an Italian–English dictionary, as they would need one to learn the language. They still held hands wherever they went, loving each other's company. The water taxi returned and whisked them back to the hotel.

The next day, they called the lady who was redecorating the villa and met with her there. They walked through the building with the decorator, making sure of the correct colors, drapes, and furnishings.

While Lilly and the decorator were standing and talking

in the master bedroom, the lady asked Lilly if she was going to decorate the patio of the master bedroom. Lilly was surprised and said, "I thought that was the roof of the recording studio."

The decorator said, "Oh, no, you have three patios: one off the master bedroom, one off the recording studio, and the one on the boat dock."

Lilly laughed and said, "I thought they were just rooftops."

The lady replied, "They serve both purposes."

Lilly said, "I want all three decorated in Mediterranean Blue and a divan glider on all three with chairs and tables." The decorator said she would take care of it. Lilly said, "Be sure to have some large live plants on each patio. I also want a drink cooler on each patio." Lilly told the lady, out of Bernard's hearing, that she wanted a sign eighteen inches by six feet naming the villa. Lilly gave her the name to be engraved, and she said she wanted the sign painted the same color as the outside blue trim, with the letters inset in gold paint and set in a black background. The sign would be a surprise, so it was not to be installed until the day of the wedding.

After checking everything in the building, Lilly asked Bernard if he had thought of anything. He said he would like two heavy floor easels for them to paint on. Lilly conveyed to the decorator to get the two heavy floor easels for the art studio. She said the recording studio would need some desks and chairs, but she would order the recording equipment later.

She asked Bernard what he thought of the place. He replied he would be out of place but that he would fit right in cutting the grass and hedges. Lilly replied, "No, we will have gardeners to do that. I also want to plant a flower garden, similar to what Betsey has but smaller."

She walked up to Bernard, put her arms around him, and looked him in the eyes. Grinning, she said, "Bernard, all of this is because of my love for you. This is a result of your love for me, and I wouldn't change anything for the world." Then she said, "The money I'm spending on this is just a pittance of what I've earned. We have the rest of our lives, so please enjoy it with me. I know it may be hard, but you have made me happy beyond belief." They kissed and walked down the stairs to the water's edge on the patio and boat dock, admiring the view.

Lilly said, "We need to go to the dressmaker and see if our clothes fit." As they were leaving, they checked in with the decorator. Lilly asked her if she understood the sign instructions, and she acknowledged that she did.

They got back into Bernard's Maserati and drove over to the tailor's and dressmaker's shop. They were greeted the only way an Italian shopkeeper can: joyfully and with a welcome. She had Bernard try on his suit, shirt, and shoes. Everything fit perfectly.

Lilly still would not let Bernard see her wedding outfit. Lilly's was also perfect after a few nips and tucks were done. The dressmaker warned her not to overeat before the wedding.

All the clothes were to be gathered up by the wedding planner and taken to the church on the day before the wedding. Mary and Betsey still had to come and get fitted for their dresses. They stopped and ate at another Italian restaurant on the way back to the hotel.

Arriving at the hotel, Bernard retrieved his painting gear from the hotel storage and made an inventory of what he had on hand. He called an order in to his supplier for paints and brushes, doubling up on the order as Lilly would be painting full time with him.

Bernard teased Lilly that he would have to be careful teaching her art, because he had fallen in love with the last pupil he taught. She in turn teased him, saying, "If you would keep your mind on the teaching instead of the female pupil, that wouldn't happen."

Bernard, laughing, said, "I was entrapped by a beautiful woman with a beautiful voice and a very enticing perfume. They use perfume like a fishing line. They throw it out there and slowly pull it back in until they catch him. Then he is powerless and cannot defend himself."

Lilly, laughing, came over to where he was writing and said, "You broke the line and went away, but I caught you again on the bank of Lake Maggiore." She then proceeded to smother him with passionate kisses. The only way he had to defend himself was to escort her into the bedroom.

The days passed quickly, and just three days until the wedding, Mary was due in with Betsey. They were to pick up a rental car and drive to the hotel. They arrived a little after three. Lilly and Bernard were waiting in their hotel suite. Hearing the doorbell, Bernard answered the door. There was Mary with Betsey. Bernard hugged both, greeting Betsey with a powerful hug and commenting on how pretty she looked. He told her if Lilly backed out of the wedding, he was going to marry her. She was elated but said, "I don't think there is any danger of Lilly backing out."

They went onto the balcony where Lilly was waiting. Lilly greeted Betsey with a hug and told her she was glad she came. Betsey, looking at the hotel and the view of Lake Maggiore, could not believe the opulence of the place. She commented that it was just like living in a palace.

While they were talking, the bellhop arrived with their luggage. Bernard had him put it next door, as they had reserved it for the wedding for Mary and Betsey. Bernard asked Betsey what she thought of the place. She came back with her famous saying, "Oh, I've never seen such a place. I think it is the most beautiful place I have ever seen."

It was his chance to tease Lilly. He told Betsey that Lilly had bought a home here, so he decided to stay here with her. Betsey started loudly laughing, saying, "I'm sure that was a hard decision for you to make."

Lilly, laughing, told Betsey, "He is going to keep on pressing his luck, and there is going to be a shooting instead of a wedding."

Betsey said, "I don't have to worry. I know how much you two love each other. I wish everyone got along as well as you two."

Lilly told Mary that her and Betsey's dresses were ready and that they would go to the dressmaker's tomorrow and then drive out to see the house. She told them she and Bernard were to spend their first night at the villa, then go on their honeymoon from there. She told them a wedding coordinator had planned the whole wedding as well as the wedding dinner, and that Mary and Betsey could stay at the hotel long as they wished. Mary said she would stay over, and she said she would take

Betsey to Isola Bella to see the palace, which she had not yet seen herself.

Bernard suggested they drive around and see the area they would be living in. Arriving down at the car, Lilly asked Mary how she liked Bernard's new car. "It was his wedding present," Lilly said, "I had to twist his arm to take it."

Mary said, "I love it."

Bernard drove them out to the villa, which was nearly completed, to show Mary and Betsey. Betsey was overcome by the beautiful countryside. On arrival, Mary and Betsey could hardly believe the beauty and size of the villa. Most of the repainting was finished. Nearly all of the furniture was in except some side tables. All the new drapes were up.

Betsey said, "This place must have cost a fortune." Bernard laughingly replied that he was going to mow and rake lawns to help pay for it. Betsey said, "You had better get busy, because it looks as though you have a lot of catching up to do."

Lilly took them through all of the house, including the bedrooms with baths and the baths in the common areas as well as the formal living and dining areas. From the master bedroom, she took them out on the patio, showing them the three patios, each stepping down from the last.

She took them through the recording studio and, last, the art studio with the two new heavy floor easels. Mary laughed and said, "We didn't live this well in London."

Lilly teasingly said, "I knew Bernard was coming into a windfall of money due to his marriage, so I thought I would spend it."

Bernard said he pleaded innocent because he did not know what he was getting into.

After all of the oohing and aahing, it was time to go. They went back to the hotel so Betsey could dine looking out over the lake. Bernard asked for and got a table next to the window with a lake view. Betsey was mesmerized by the place. Betsey told Lilly, "I am sure glad Bernard stuck his head through that hedge because of all the nice things you have done for me that I never could have done on my own. Inviting me to be part of the wedding!—I still can't believe it."

Lilly replied, "There is no one more deserving than you and no one we would rather have than you."

After they had finished a delightful meal, it was getting dark and the lights began to flicker on the lake. Bernard said, "Let us go upstairs so Betsey can see the lake at night." The view from the balcony took Betsey's breath away. She remarked that she had never seen such a beautiful sight.

They had a happy gathering and talked until bedtime. Mary and Betsey went to the next-door suite with the understanding that they would eat breakfast together.

The next morning, they gathered in Lilly and Bernard's suite and had breakfast brought up on a cart. This was all new to Betsey, eating on a balcony and watching the boats go by. After their leisurely breakfast, they met downstairs at the car. They drove out to the dressmaker's so Mary and Betsey could try on their dresses. The dresses only needed a little adjustment, and their shoes fit properly. The lady said they could be picked up tomorrow, the day of the wedding. Lilly said the wedding planner would pick them up.

They drove out to check on the villa. Everything was

complete except for some sweeping and vacuuming. Mary thought everything was fantastic. Lilly told her she could stay in London and run things there or move in with them. "You could go ahead and get married," Lilly said. "I have no plans to go back to London except for legal situations. The condominium is yours, and I will deed it to you."

They met with the wedding planner to finalize the proceedings. The wedding planner asked if Lilly was going to walk down the aisle. Lilly replied, "No. I've had two weddings, and this one is not for show, but to honor the man I am marrying."

Lilly wanted a song played that she had recorded. She would come out from the left side of the pulpit, and Bernard would come out from the right side and wait for her. She would stop about two feet from Bernard and wait until her song to finish. That would be her devotion to him. The musicians would play, and the singer would sing the words to "The Wedding Promise." That would be Bernard's devotion to her.

Then the preacher would say the wedding vows with Bernard and Lilly, and that would be it. As it was to be a small wedding and they had ordered plenty of food, Lilly would invite everyone to come to the wedding dinner.

The wedding would start at half past three. After the wedding, they would leave the church and go to the Grand Hotel Bristol, where they had reserved a private room where they would have the wedding dinner and the musicians would be playing Lilly's most popular songs.

Bernard suggested they get a quick lunch, for he had arranged for a private boat ride at two p.m. They stopped at a restaurant and had a quick meal in order to meet the boat. They met the boat at the hotel dock. That dock would be more convenient when the ride ended, as they would be at the hotel.

While waiting on the boat to arrive, they told Betsey this was the place Lilly found Bernard painting, and they said he also had proposed at that very spot. Betsey was amazed because she had been instrumental in them being together. The boat arrived, and everyone boarded. It was a luxury boat with very plush seating. The boat operator took them around several islands and past the luxury homes along the lake, including a ride by their new villa. It looked beautiful from the water. Bernard asked Betsey how she liked the boat ride. She said, "I see why you want to live here. It is such a beautiful place."

They were back at the boat dock by five o'clock. Everyone enjoyed the ride, and they were glad to be back on dry land.

Bernard directed them into the restaurant for the evening meal. They ordered their meals, and the chatter began. Everyone had something exciting to tell about what they had seen on the boat ride.

Betsey, having lived a somewhat sheltered life, was overwhelmed by it all: the hotel, the lake, the scenery, and the new home. They took their time eating and finished around 6:30. Then they deciding to go up to their suites. They sat out on Lilly's balcony talking and admiring the house lights on the lake.

This continued until 10:30, when Bernard called it a night for everyone because of the big day tomorrow.

Mary and Betsey went on to their suite, leaving Lilly and Bernard sitting and holding onto each other. At midnight, they called it a day and turned in. They both had a restless sleep during the night because of the anticipation of the wedding.

The next morning, they wandered in one by one for breakfast. Bernard had already placed the order. The food arrived at about the same time Lilly arrived. Most wanted juice to start, then some hot tea, while Bernard took coffee. They had a huge variety of food. Each of them ate at a leisurely pace.

Lilly recommended that they go to the church to make sure everything was in order. After that, they would have a leisurely lunch till about two p.m., then back to the church to get dressed for the wedding.

No one seemed to be in a hurry. They were able to be dressed just past ten a.m. They went to the church to make sure all their clothes were there, including their shoes. Satisfied everything was in order, they continued to the villa and see if it was completed.

Lilly and Bernard were to spend their honeymoon night at the villa and depart the next morning on their honeymoon. When they arrived at the villa, the outside was a showpiece in itself. They entered the building to find a beautifully decorated house. Bernard and Lilly were very pleased. They went down to the dock and sat on the patio chairs. They all agreed that the place was a delight.

Lilly asked Mary to check the refrigerator for drinks for everyone. The house decorator was supposed to get a variety of drinks and stock several refrigerators. She had also hired a maid for them who would start the day before they returned from their honeymoon. That way, everything would be clean for them.

After noon, Bernard said it was time to eat. Everyone loaded into the car, and Bernard drove them to a nice restaurant. They finished their meal in about an hour and a half, and he drove them to the church to start getting dressed for the wedding. Mary's and Betsey's dresses were identical mid-calf length. They were long-sleeved and in a medium shade of mauve. They had a light shade of lace on the bodice and sleeve areas and dark mauve matching sashes and large bows tied in back, with tails down to knee length. They wore light mauve hose and dark mauve pumps. This was topped off with mid-tone mauve biscuit hats with light mauve netting down to the eyes.

Bernard's suit was dark blue with a light mauve shirt and a dark mauve tie, dark mauve socks, and black shoes. Bernard's boutonniere and Mary and Betsey's corsages were lily-of-the-valley with mauve ribbons.

Lilly's dress was waltz length in ivory, with lace on the bodice area and wrist-length sleeves with real pearl buttons down the front. The dress had a net overskirt of light mauve with a dark mauve sash. The butterfly broach rested on her left chest. She wore a biscuit hat of ivory color with light mauve nose-length netting and real pearls sewn into the netting. An ivory veil was attached to the back of the biscuit hat and extended down to the large dark-mauve bow in the back. The bride's bouquet was lily-of-the-valley and purple violets attached to the ten parchment letters. Light mauve hose and dark mauve pumps completed her wedding attire.

Betsey was the ring bearer and would stand next to Bernard. Mary was the bridesmaid and would give the bride away.

While they were getting into their wedding dresses, Mary knew how sentimental Lilly had become around Bernard, and she asked her if she would be all right during the ceremony. Lilly, sounding chipper and making light of the subject, said, "This is my third one. I am an old soldier at this. I've got it down pat."

Mary was not so sure. Lilly would spar with her first two husbands in a flash, but there was something different with Bernard. She likes to tease him but never got over telling him he was too old. Just the thought or mention of it brought her to tears. She never wanted to hurt him again.

Seeing the love he expressed to her each day while they were painting really drew her into him. She had never experienced love from a man as from Bernard, since her father had been killed in the war. Mary had the feeling that if anyone were to cross Bernard when Lilly was around, there would be hell to pay.

Now, with just thirty minutes before the wedding was to start, Mary told Betsey to go over to Bernard's side, as she would accompany him on the way out. They were to wait until the recording of Lily singing started.

The musicians had been playing soft music until it was time to start. When Betsey arrived, Bernard gave her the ring. The music started for Lilly's song "Can't Help Falling In Love," so Bernard and Betsey walked out and took their places. After the first verse played, Lilly walked in, took her place, and started singing her song to Bernard.

Bernard could not believe how beautiful she was in her dress, holding a bridal bouquet of violets and lily-of-the-valley with a mauve bow attached on top of ten parchment love letters. This is the woman he had fallen in love with just at hearing her songs. His eyes began to moisten. Surely, he thought, men do not cry at their weddings.

Lilly, singing her song of her love for Bernard, noticed how good-looking he was. After she finished her song, they moved within two feet of each other and waited for the singer to sing the song Bernard had written to Lilly. He called it "The Wedding Promise." Lilly had not heard it because it was a surprise from Bernard. It was written to the music of "Serenade to Spring" by Secret Garden. The musicians began to play the lead-in to the song, and then the singer began to sing:

> *In the garden of love, I will give you my Troth*
> *and I'll love you forevermore.*
> *As our Future begins and we promise*
> *our love and I give you my hand forevermore.*
> *As I give you my hand and my trust in your*
> *Love I betroth my heart to you.*

Lilly, upon hearing the words of the song, had tears beginning to run down her face. The man she had told was too old was pouring his heart out in song. The song continued:

> *As I give you my hand, would you please*
> *Understand, I will ever belong to you.*
> *Will, you ever be True to the love*
> *I've for you and forever be true to me?*
> *And Forever be told of my love to behold*
> *And forever and ever belong to me.*

Lilly could not stand it any longer. She walked over to Bernard, put her arm around his waist, and put her head on his chest. Bernard put his arm around her and said, "It is all right. Everything will be all right," holding her tight. The song continued:

> *As I give you my hand, will you please*
> *Understand my heart belongs to you*
> *Forever my love I bequeath you*
> *My heart and I'll ever belong in your arms.*
> *Will, you ever be mine for the rest*
> *Of your life and I will to you.*
> *As we're joined in our love for the*
> *Rest of our lives, I will ever belong to*
> *You—I will ever belong to you.*[3]

Mary, with tears in her eyes, leaned over and gave Lilly a handkerchief. Betsey and Bernard both had tears in their eyes. The minister waited a few minutes for everyone to get some composure. Then, wiping tears from his eyes, he began to speak. "I have performed weddings for almost forty years, and I have never seen as much love between two people as I have here today." He asked who was giving the bride away.

Mary said, "I am."

He went on having them to exchange their vows. He asked for the ring. Betsey gave him the ring. He had Bernard place the

---

3 Secret Garden. "Serenade to Spring." In *Songs from a Secret Garden.* Rolf Løvland, 1995, CD. Published May 24, 2018 on Secret Garden's official YouTube channel at https://youtu.be/87s99PUdaGg

ring on Lilly's finger, then asked for the man's ring, and Mary gave him the ring. He had Lilly place the ring on Bernard's finger. Then he finished his ceremony and pronounced them man and wife, saying, "You may kiss the bride."

Everyone was all smiles, and they congratulated the newly married couple. Lilly and Bernard announced that everyone present (a few tourists had wandered in) were invited to the wedding dinner at the Grand Hotel Bristol. Bernard and Lilly had a limousine pick them up, and Mary drove Bernard's car back to the hotel.

When the limousine neared the hotel, Lilly told Bernard she wanted to get out at the park bench. Bernard had the driver stop near the bench. After they got out, he told the driver to go on. Lilly and Bernard walked over and sat down on the bench. They sat for a few moments not saying anything.

Then Lilly spoke. "This place means so much to me. Everything good that had ever happened in my life has happened here. That is why I wanted to live and get married here." She looked at Bernard and said, "I love you so much it hurts. Every day when I look at you, I know how blessed I am having you. I think of what I would have missed if I had not found you. Then you wrote that wedding promise. In that song today, you poured your heart out to me, and I could see the heartbreak when I told you were too old. I am so sorry I did that, though I did not mean it."

Bernard said, "Lilly, forget that forever. I felt the same way. I still loved you, although I was disappointed. That song I wrote was to reinforce the feelings I have for you. Lilly, today is a new beginning. Exchanging vows today was for us to be committed to each other for the rest of our lives. Every day, I look at you and marvel at what you see in me, a dirt farmer from the hills of Tennessee."

"Oh, Bernard, you are blinded looking at yourself. You do not see what we women see in you, and I am glad of that. Remember, Betsey said any woman would like to have a man like you."

Bernard said, "We need to get over to the hotel. We are holding them up." They got up, and Bernard embraced her and told her how happy he was to spend the rest of his life with her. Then he kissed her endearingly.

When they arrived at the hotel, everyone was greeting them and congratulating them. Entering the wedding reception room, everyone there greeted them. They asked for a speech. Bernard said, "I don't have much to say. All I know is I was on my way to tour Europe, minding my own business, and at my first stop I got distracted." Everyone laughed, knowing falling in love and marrying Lilly is what had distracted him.

Lilly said, "When he found out I had marriage on my mind, he ran off, and I had to chase him down." They all had a good laugh and enjoyed the wonderful meal.

At the cake cutting, Mary took the top layer and saved it for when they got back from their honeymoon. Cutting the cake for themselves, they each took a bite of each other's cake. They had so much love and respect for each other, they did not try to cram and smear cake over each other.

Bernard called for the limousine and bid everyone good night. They told Betsey goodbye, because they would not see her again before she went back home. On the way to their villa, they held hands and reflected on their experiences over the past year.

The limousine arrived at their villa, and Bernard told the driver to pick them up at ten a.m. the next day. Bernard got out first and waited on Lilly. Taking his hand, she walked him over to the side of the yard near the street and pointed at a black and gold sign with Mediterranean Blue trim. The sign read, "Villa Monterey." Bernard was flabbergasted, saying, "What on Earth?"

Lilly said, "It's a surprise for you. I named it after your hometown."

Bernard was almost brought to tears. He said, "Oh, Lilly, I can never catch up with you."

Lilly said, "You are not supposed to. I didn't want you to get homesick."

Every time Bernard turned around, Lilly was doing something nice for him. He hugged and kissed her, holding her for a few moments. He said, "What can I do for you?"

"Tell me you love me, that's all. Now I would like you to carry me into the house."

Bernard said, "That I can do." Picking her up after unlocking the door, he carried her into the house. He put her down and said, "How's that, Mrs. Anderson?"

"Just fine," she smiled, and she said, "Honey, we are home."

Bernard smiled and said, "That we are!"

Chapter 9

Lilly looked Bernard in the eyes and said, "Welcome to Villa Monterey!"

Bernard became very humble and told Lilly she was the most thoughtful and unselfish person he ever knew.

Lilly replied, "I took art lessons from a very wise sage, and he taught me these things."

He replied, "Lilly, you give me too much credit."

Lilly said, "Let us get out of these clothes. I want to relax down on the patio by the lake before bedtime."

They went into their master bedroom and had to take their bed clothing from the suitcases, as they had not transferred their clothes over to the villa. Lilly asked Bernard to unclasp her pearl necklace and the back snap on her wedding dress. She took off her dress while Bernard was taking off his suit, and there, underneath her wedding dress, Lilly had on a fancy lace mauve push-up bra with a matching half slip trimmed in lace. She removed the half slip to reveal matching short-leg panties trimmed in lace with an embroidered heart on the right side.

Bernard said, "Lilly, please put on your robe."

Giggling, she answered, "Why?"

He replied, "If you don't, we will not make it past the bed on the way down to the patio."

Lilly laughed and said, "I was just checking to see if your hormones were still working."

"Right now, they are on overload."

Lilly put her robe on over her bra and panties, then put on her slippers. Bernard put on his pajamas and slippers, and they went down to the patio by the water. Bernard poured each of them a glass of champagne from the patio refrigerator. They sat on the well-upholstered glider Lilly had required the house decorator to order for her. Bernard sat on the end, and Lilly sat next to him, pulling her feet and legs up under her. She leaned over on Bernard's chest as he put his arm around her. Admiring the beautiful view of the lake, Lilly said, "Now this is what I call a real honeymoon. I did not want it to be too commercial by traveling to a hotel somewhere and having to rush through the honeymoon. However, every day since I found you here in Stresa has been a honeymoon for me."

Lilly, forever being the teaser, told Bernard how wonderful he was and said, "I have only one disappointment in you."

"What's that?" said Bernard.

"I found out that you steal."

"Lilly, I don't know what you are talking about. I don't steal."

"Yes, you do. I can tell you when it happened. Do you remember back when we were painting, I asked how you and your landlady got along? You said, 'Who, Betsey?' I said yes, and you said, 'She's family; she's not a landlady.' I could see the compassion you had for other people. That is when you stole my heart. I knew then if you could call someone family whom you paid to live there, you were the man for me."

Bernard, catching on to the joke, said, "Do you want me to give it back?"

"No, you have been nurturing it very well, so I decided if it means that much to you, you can keep it."

"Oh, Lilly, I love you so much," he replied, and he put both arms around her. "I'm glad you decided to spend our first night here at our little paradise. You should have named this place Paradise, instead of Monterey."

She replied, "No, you are a part of me, and Monterey is a part of you. We can still have a paradise here in Villa Monterey." Then Lilly said, "Oh, listen, they are playing mandolin music. Isn't it romantic?"

After an hour of resting and loving, Lilly said, "It's time to go up and consummate the marriage." Bernard, joking said, "Well, I will try to do my part."

Lilly smiled, looked at Bernard, and said, "Honey, you have been doing a pretty good job of your part for about three weeks." Bernard just smiled.

Arriving in the bedroom, Lilly said, "Shall I change into my sheer nightgown?"

"Oh no," said Bernard, "you've done enough damage with the bra and panties you have on."

Lilly giggled and slid under the covers with Bernard right beside her. After Lilly and Bernard consummated the marriage, Lilly turned her back toward Bernard to rest in his arms, thinking how happy she was with his arms around her. Home at last, she shed tears of happiness upon her pillow. This was her first "feel-at-home house" since she had been taken to live with her grandparents. She remembered the many nights she cried herself to sleep, missing her father and then her mother. It was nice being there with her mother's parents, but it was not home, although it helped to have her cousin Mary for company.

Thinking about their honeymoon trip that was to start the following day, she was having second thoughts. She did not want to leave this villa to go on a honeymoon, but she did not want to disappoint Bernard and have him think that she thought less of him. She felt she could spend the rest of her life here at Villa Monterey, and it would be like a honeymoon forever. She decided she would go as planned, but she dreaded leaving the villa. Even though there were things to do and places to see in Paris, nothing could compare with her villa and the surroundings of Lake Maggiore. After a while, she drifted off to sleep. The next morning, they both were slow to move. Lilly got up first and was slow to move around, dreading to leave her villa that she loved so much. She told Bernard they had better shower and dress, as the limousine would be here at ten a.m. to take them to the airport. They both bathed, then went to the kitchen, where Mary had left some sweet rolls for them. Lilly made tea, being British, and Bernard made coffee for himself. They quickly ate, and Bernard started closing the suitcases to carry them out the front door. He noticed Lilly was moving slowly, and he had to hurry her to get her suitcases repacked so he could get them out front in time for the limousine.

The limousine arrived shortly, and the driver loaded the suitcases into the limousine. On the way to the airport, Lilly was quiet, and did not talk much; Bernard had to make most of the conversation. Waiting to board the flight to Paris, Lilly was still not very talkative. Bernard was concerned but thought she was exhausted because of the preparations for the wedding. She perked up a little when they arrived in Paris. She had been there several times, but she was glad for Bernard, as he had only been there one time.

Mary had booked them into a fine hotel near the Eiffel Tower and the center of the attractions. They had spent the biggest part of the day traveling and decided just to walk around a few blocks from the hotel. After unpacking, they went outside and walked the streets, enjoying Paris. They found a nice restaurant and ate their evening meal. They took their time getting back to the hotel. Arriving back in their room, they enjoyed looking at the lights of Paris from the high windows of their hotel room. Lilly warmed up to Bernard considerably.

The next day they went to the Palace of Versailles and marveled at the opulence of the Hall of Mirrors, the beautiful palace, and the manicured grounds. They spent the next day at the Church of Notre Dame and at Sainte-Chappelle, the church of the king of France. This was one place Lilly had never been. She could not get over the three sides of the church with windows of all colors of glass and figures that went from floor to ceiling. There were over eleven hundred windows, and some of them were about forty-five feet high. The downstairs was decorated similar to a harem, very colorful and very beautiful.

The following day, Bernard wanted Lilly to see the paint stalls where the painters of Paris painted and sold their paintings. The Moulin Rouge was on the street just below Montmartre, with its overlook of Paris, and the Sacré-Coeur Basilica. They went to the paint stalls first, and Lilly was excited to see the artists at work. She bought two paintings of Paris landmarks.

They sat on the steps of Sacré-Coeur for about half an hour. Bernard could tell something was bothering Lilly. Finally, Lilly said, "Bernard, I want to go home to Monterey."

"To our villa?" asked Bernard.

"Yes," she said.

Bernard asked if she was feeling okay.

"Yes," she replied.

He said, "We have four more days left here."

"I don't care. I want to go home."

When they got back to the hotel, Bernard called the airlines and booked a flight for the next day. They packed up their suitcases, except for their nightclothes and the clothes they would wear the next day. They turned in early and requested a wake-up call.

The next morning, they had breakfast in their room, had a bellhop put the luggage outside, and hailed a cab to the airport. Lilly held Bernard's hand on the flight back to Italy. On landing, they got a chauffeur take them back to their villa. On arrival at their Villa, they had the chauffeur set the luggage inside, and Bernard paid the chauffeur.

Lilly took Bernard by the hand and walked him over to the Villa Monterey sign she had had made for him. Putting her arm around him, she asked him again how he liked it. He told her he loved it.

She led him over to the front door and said, "Bernard, would you carry me over the threshold again? It would mean so much to me."

Bernard said, "I will be delighted." He picked her up,

carried her across the threshold, then took his foot and kicked the door closed. As he put her down inside, she began to cry, saying, "I'm home."

Bernard, knowing she was upset about something said, "Lilly, if you are having second thoughts about our marriage, I will understand."

She looked at him and said, "Bernard, don't you ever think that again. I didn't want to go on a honeymoon. I did not know how to tell you, but I went because of you. When we spent our first night here, I felt at home for the first time since I was six years old and my mother took me to live with my grandparents. That was not home. I did not feel at home in my marriages. Even my condominium did not feel like home. But when I married you and we spent our first night here, I felt at home for the first time in twenty-six years. That is why I hated to go on a honeymoon. I knew it would not feel the same."

Looking at Bernard through her tears, she said, "Bernard, you are my home, and Villa Monterey is my home. I do not want to ever leave here, and I want to start our family. I did not know I was missing this part of my life until I met you. You have completely turned my life around, and I am thankful for that. You just do not know how much I love you."

Bernard picked her up, carried her into the bedroom, placed her on the bed, and took off her high-heeled shoes. Taking off his shoes, he lay down beside her and embraced her in his arms.

Epilogue

Ten and a half months later, a boy from the telegraph company was ringing the bell on the front door of Betsey's house. After ringing several times and getting no answer, he decided to go around to the back of the house, and he saw Betsey working in the garden. He yelled hello to get her attention and started walking toward her. She, in turn, walked out of her garden carrying her hoe with her. She met the young man at the little green garage. He handed her the telegram, and she thanked him. She could not imagine who could be sending her a telegram. She opened the envelope and read:

MR. AND MRS. BERNARD ANDERSON ARE PROUD TO ANNOUNCE THE ARRIVAL OF BETTY "BETSEY" MAUVENA ANDERSON INTO THE WORLD AT 04:10 AM STRESA TIME. EIGHT POUNDS FOUR OUNCES, NINETEEN INCHES LONG. COME QUICK. NEED HELP. MARY WILL CALL AND BRING YOU. LOVE, BERNARD

Betsey, talking to herself, said, "Oh, they have a little girl."